THE COLOUR OF HEAVEN

James Runcie is a writer and film-maker. His first novel, *The Discovery of Chocolate*, was published to great acclaim and his films include *Heaven*, *The Great Fire*, *My Father*, *Saturday/Sunday*, *Miss Pym's Day Out* and *Childhood*.

Praise for THE DISCOVERY OF CHOCOLATE:

'A sensual delight . . . elegantly written and unashamed fun'   JOANNE HARRIS

'As intoxicating and addictive as the substance it describes. The novel is a triumph of inspired imagination'   *Financial Times*

'A work of engaging simplicity which reads well, has plenty of light and shade and never patronises the reader. The potent appeal of chocolate . . . is vividly captured. Mouth-watering descriptions of food litter the text'   *Sunday Telegraph*

'His treasure of a book, fantastic and delicious and dreamily erotic by turns, will transmute your yearning for the bitter water into a craving from which you will, quite happily, never recover'   SIMON WINCHESTER, author of *The Surgeon of Crowthorne*

D1076605

By the same author

The Discovery of Chocolate

JAMES RUNCIE

THE COLOUR OF HEAVEN

TED SMART

This novel is a work of fiction.
The names, characters and incidents portrayed in it
are the work of the author's imagination.
Any resemblance to actual persons, living or dead,
events or localities is entirely coincidental.

This edition produced for The Book People Ltd,
Hall Wood Avenue, Haydock, St Helens WA11 9UL

HarperCollins*Publishers*
77–85 Fulham Palace Road,
Hammersmith, London W6 8JB

www.harpercollins.co.uk

Published by HarperCollins*Publishers* 2003
1 3 5 7 9 8 6 4 2

A catalogue record for this book
is available from the British Library

ISBN 0 00 770559 X

Set in PostScript Linotype Giovanni by
Rowland Phototypesetting Ltd,
Bury St Edmunds, Suffolk

Printed and bound in Great Britain by
Clays Ltd, St Ives plc

for Marilyn

Tazata
Taingin
Mongol.
Naiman
Mongul
Coßin
Cattigara
Cam- balich
Tenduc.
obij fl.
Turfon
Campi on.
Ca thaio
ch
Kitai lac
Cotam
Singui.
Gouza
S. ach.
I
A
Xibuar
Paskent
Congu
Tangiu
fi
Turcheltan
Caraxan
Camdu.
Quanzu
Samarchand
Voci: am
Iaci
China.
Quinzai
raian
Danm
Amu.
Carsi.
Turbet.
Candahar
Chesi- mur.
Baicon del
Bonpria
Iatim
Li
hestan.
Serchis.
Mien
zaita
Guzarate
India orien
Aua
Cantan.
Calama- tx
Arda man
Man dao
Caoi
talis.
Lichi
Delli
Tame ri.
Deitan
Indhu fl.
Cam bau
Orixa
Brema
Tinha
Goa
Cape lan
Narsiga
Malaca
Cah oia
Pulo
Calecut
atalia mir
Carigam
Pulo sirsir
y di Mal: diuar
Como
Caldea
Zeilan
Su
mano pe
Gißam
matra
ancesco.
Due Compagne.
Iaua ma ior
Don Garçia
Poueada

No jewel is worth his lady

Sapphire, nor diamond, nor emerald,
Nor other precious stones past reckoning,
Topaz, nor pearl, nor ruby like a king,
Nor that most virtuous jewel, jasper call'd,
Nor amethyst, nor onyx, nor basalt,
Each counted for a very marvellous thing,
Is half so excellently gladdening
As is my lady's head uncoronall'd.
All beauty by her beauty is made dim;
Like to the stars she is for loftiness;
And with her voice she taketh away grief.
She is fairer than a bud, or than a leaf.
Christ have her well in keeping, of His grace,
And make her holy and beloved, like Him!

Jacopo da Lentino, 1250
Translated by Dante Gabriel Rossetti

VENICE

No one noticed the child.

He had been left in a small boat which now sailed out towards the lagoon, following nothing but the slap and tide of each narrow canal.

It was Ascension Day in the year twelve hundred and ninety-five, and the people of Venice were parading through the streets, hoisting crimson pennants and bright-yellow banners in celebration. Tailors dressed in white tunics with crimson stars, weavers in silver cloth tippets, and cotton spinners in cloaks of fustian mingled with blacksmiths, carpenters, butchers, and bakers, singing and shouting their way towards the Piazza San Marco.

The square was filled with showmen, swindlers, sooth-sayers, and charlatans; jesters, jugglers, prophets, and priests. Alchemists cried out that scrapings of amber gave protection from the plague, and that an emerald pressed against naked flesh could preserve a woman from apoplexy. A dentist with silver teeth sold a special compound which he vowed would improve the value of all metal; a barber displayed a gum to make bald men hirsute; and a naked Englishman sold pine seeds which were said to guarantee invisibility as surely as the talisman of Gyges.

But no one had noticed the baby.

Teresa could have ignored him, another abandoned child due for an early death at the Foundlings' Hospital; but once she had seen him the shock of love took hold.

She watched the boat spin gently against the side of a little *rio*, caught in a momentary eddy, as if waiting only for her arrival. Perhaps this was a gift from God at last, alleviation for all that she had suffered.

She looked around, for mother or father, doctor or stranger, but amidst the movement of the crowd they were the only people to be still, the abandoned baby and the woman who could never have children: Teresa, wife of Marco the glass-maker, barren. No other adjective was necessary. Her pale-blue eyes, thin frame, and slender beauty meant nothing. When people wanted to describe her, they spoke but the one word: barren.

She knelt down beside the waters and gathered in the child.

'*Calme, calme, mio bambino.*'

The baby's mouth began to pucker, longing for milk.

Teresa knew that she should go into the church and ask the priest what to do but at that moment the doors swung open and a vast procession emerged, singing Psalms and praising God. She let the pageant go by, watching a group of children carrying silver bowls filled with rose petals, whispering and squabbling as they passed.

Teresa tried to convince herself that she did not need the child. She should leave him, as his mother had left him, and as hundreds of other mothers would do on this very day throughout the city. Children were a drain, and a curse, the punishment for sexual excess. They cried. They were always hungry. They grew up to take your money and denounce you. That was what Marco had always told her: her husband, who could, in fact, be as barren as she. They had never known.

She could hear his voice telling her to put the baby back, leaving it either for charity, another mother, or death. What was one child more or one child less in the world when we are born only to live, suffer, and die?

She sat down on the steps of the church.

The child was so pale and so fair.

ॐ

Out in the lagoon, trumpeters, troubadours, and drummers sailed past the Doges' Palace singing of beauty and lost love, saluting both the rising and the setting of the sun, mothers and daughters, mistresses and maids, the besotted and the beloved.

Some of the boats were preparing tableaux of the Christian mysteries: the shipwrights and carpenters were to re-enact Noah's flood; the vintners would create the illusion of Christ turning the water into wine, whereas Marco's single-sailed *sandolo* had been transformed into a moveable theatre in which his fellow glass-makers would perform 'The harrowing of hell'.

His friends were dressed as heavy-drinking devils with horns made from old fish baskets, and their blowpipes had become instruments of diabolic torture. Marco was to play the devil himself. He stood on the prow, his smoky frame dominating the boat, and bellowed a list of the torments awaiting all sinners. Rival guilds watched in wonder as Marco blew flames, drank, shouted, and sang of terror and disaster. The nearer other boats sailed, the more dramatic his gestures became until he could resist temptation no longer and began to describe the precise location of the mouth of hell.

He turned round, bent over, and mooned at all who might look at him, shouting:

> *'Guarda! Guarda!*
> *La bocca d'inferno è nel mio culo!'*

Encouraged by his companions, he then provided a triumphant auditory accompaniment to the gesture.

'Ecco un fracasso del diavolo!'

The longer the day lasted, and the more red wine they drank, the funnier such antics seemed, until the time came for the youngest glass-maker to harrow hell. Young Pietro emerged from beneath the sail (which now became the flag of Resurrection) carrying a vast glass crucifix and shouted:

'We have blown this crucifix as surely as Christ will blast away the gates of Death.'

He then struck his fellow workers with the cross, and they dived into the waters of the lagoon, an improbable reminder of the power of baptism and redemption.

'This sky is our heaven, these waters our home. Let no one deny the promises we have been vouchsafed!' Pietro shouted.

The Doge's gilded barge, the *Bucintoro*, sailed past the spluttering glass-makers in preparation for the ceremonial marriage of Venice to the sea. The boat moved out towards the Lido, canopied in red, shining with golden river gods, zephyrs, putti, and mermaids, the Lion of St Mark fluttering above.

The Doge rose to the prow of his ship and took the ceremonial glass ring from his finger.

Then he proclaimed, '*O Sea, we wed thee in sign of our everlasting dominion*,' and threw the ring out into the Adriatic.

The *Bucintoro* turned back, its oars gleaming in the light. Marco and his men, now safely back on board their boat, raised a *fiasco* of wine, as if toasting their leader, and prepared to sail back to Murano, content with their day's display.

༄

As they did so, Teresa opened her blouse and pinched at her breast. The child squirmed in her arms. She would have to take the baby to her sister, for, whereas Teresa could not even begin to conceive, Francesca could not stop having children. The milk poured out of her so much that she worked as a wet nurse to sustain her family.

Teresa began to walk up towards the Misericordia. She watched the crowd stream over the bridges, returning home to eat and drink before the curfew, ready to share their thoughts about the day, to joke perhaps, to laugh, even to make love.

Boats headed out into the lagoon.

At first her sister thought she was carrying the baby on a mission from another mother. 'Where is it from?'

'I do not know.'

'What have you done?'

'I have a child at last.'

'How?'

Teresa tried to remain defiant. 'I found it. By the Church of the Apostles.'

Francesca could not believe such folly. 'If I had known you were desperate you could have raised one of mine.'

'I didn't want one of yours. I wanted one of my own.'

'Is it a boy or a girl?'

'I don't know.'

'You didn't check? Here. Let me look.'

Teresa handed her sister the child.

'It's a boy. He needs feeding.' Francesca opened her blouse and took the baby to her breast. He drank noisily, hungrily. Teresa watched the child suck and felt the first stirrings of jealousy.

'I always knew you would do something stupid.'

'It's not stupid. Look at him.'

'You'll have to pay me,' Francesca demanded.

The two sisters looked at the child, feeding greedily, possessed by need. Teresa was surprised for the first time by the noise: the spluttering and the gasping, the desire and the power of a baby at the breast sucking for life itself. 'Does it hurt?' she asked.

'Of course it does. But you get used to it. He's feeding well. Then he'll be sick.'

'Sick?'

'You've been spared all this: the milk and pain of motherhood, the jealous husband, the cries in the night. Disease. Illness. Death. What do you want a child for?'

'Joy,' said Teresa. 'I want him for joy.'

ༀ

Marco had drunk several flasks of wine by the time he rowed alongside the Fondamenta Santa Caterina to collect his wife. At times he could not believe that he was married to this woman. He wondered whether he should have wed her sister, a woman with plenty of flesh on her, proper breasts, firm hips, and a body in which a man could lose himself. But did he want all those babies and all that milk? He held his flask of wine aloft in greeting.

Teresa shivered nervously, and gave him a small wave. That is my husband, she thought, as if the events of the day had made them strangers both to the city and to each other. They had never looked as if they belonged together: Teresa thin, anxious, and bird-like; her husband broad, swarthy, and muscular, like Vulcan or some dark river god.

'Did you watch?' he asked.

Teresa had forgotten that she might have to lie. 'There were so many people. And you were far away.'

'I told you that you should have come with us.'

'There was not room. It was for men. You know that.'

'It would not have mattered.'

'Did you see the Doge?' asked Teresa.

'I did. And he saw us. It was a triumph.'

As her husband recounted the story of the day, Teresa realised that she could not take in what he was saying. She could think only of the child. Perhaps she should tell him now, she thought, in this stillness, out in the lagoon. She should confess, or even shout out, that the baby was the only thing that mattered to her, more important than either his love or her own death.

She wondered what it would be like to tell him. She almost wanted to laugh with the joy of it all, sharing this new happiness with the man she loved. But she knew that Marco would be fearful, his mood would change, and that it would ruin the day. He would talk about money. He would ask her to take the child back. And he would not give the real reason for his fear: the fact that a son might change their marriage, that they would no longer be alone.

He put out a line and began to fish.

As the boat rocked on the water, Teresa remembered

holding the child in her arms. Although she ached for him, she knew that she must hide the fact, as if the revelation of such a secret would only destroy its beauty.

At last there was movement on the line and Marco flicked up a sturgeon, its back gleaming against the dying light, twitching in midair before being cast down onto the floor of the boat.

'*E basta*,' Marco cried, still happy.

A wind started up, blowing across the lagoon. Teresa watched her husband pull in the line and begin to row harder for the island.

'Did you gather the wood this morning?' he asked.

Teresa knew the question mattered, but could not remember why. 'Alder,' she replied.

'Enough for tonight and tomorrow?'

'Plenty,' Teresa answered.

'Then I am happy.'

They tied up the *sandolo*, and Marco took his wife's hand. Together they walked along the Fondamenta dei Vetrai, past the furnaces of each family of glass-makers, lined in rivalry and solidarity, until they reached their home, glowing against the impending night, the secret unspoken between them.

ನಿ

Teresa visited her sister every week. Francesca taught her to hold the baby, calm him when he cried, rock and console him. But Teresa didn't need encouragement. As she held the boy she realised that not only was the child beginning to belong to her, but that she belonged to the child. She had given herself away.

'You look as if you've never seen a baby before,' her sister remarked.

'I haven't. Not like this.'

Teresa inspected every finger and toe. She felt the weight of her new son's head, cupping it in her palm. His eyes stared away into the distance as if he had come from some other world and knew its secrets. How could she live with such a love? How could she ever do enough for him? What if he was too hot, too cold, too hungry, or too thirsty? How could she guard against fever? What if he fell sick? What if he died?

Soon Teresa could not bear to be apart from the boy. Only she loved him sufficiently to protect him from the perils of the earth. Only she knew what it was to truly love and care for him. The anxiety grew so strong that she began to panic every time she had to leave.

'You love him too much,' Francesca warned, but Teresa insisted, 'One can never love too much.'

Her sister could not agree. 'You can. Believe me.'

Teresa could sense her disapproval.

'You had freedom. Why lose it?' Francesca continued.

'Because I need to love.'

'And the child?'

'The child would have died.'

'The hospital would have taken him.'

'You know that's a lie. And if they had . . . You know what happens. They never live.'

Francesca dismissed her sister. 'It's only a child.'

'What?'

'Some live, some die.'

'How can you be so heartless?'

'Because I know what it is to love too much.'

'Then you live in sadness.'

'At least I do not live in dread,' Francesca said quietly. 'When will you tell Marco?'

'When I bring the boy home.'

'You will not warn him?'

'No. I want there to be no argument.'

ನಌ

Marco lived a life of certainties: work, faith, and marriage. Most of the complexities of existence could be explained either by reason or by fate, and so, when he saw Teresa carrying the child, he was convinced that she was holding a new niece or nephew.

'Francesca?' he asked. 'She can't stop.'

'The child has come from Francesca but she is not the mother.'

'Who is?' He smiled. 'Have you stolen him?'

'Nobody knows.'

'Then what are you doing?'

'I want to keep him,' Teresa said suddenly.

'He's not ours to keep.' Surely she was joking.

'I found him,' she continued quietly. 'Six months ago. On Ascension Day.'

'And what have you done?'

'Francesca has weaned him for me.'

'Then Francesca can keep him.'

'No.'

It was the first time she had ever denied him.

Marco stepped back. 'You've always intended to keep him – without talking to me, without asking my permission?'

'I meant to tell you, but I knew that you would be angry.'

Why could he not understand? Did he not remember how she had been mad with the lack of a child? 'I have to keep him. He is a son. For both of us.'

'Not mine.'

'Please,' she appealed, and then immediately regretted the fact that she sounded so keen to appease.

'Give him to the priest. Or to another mother. Take him back to your sister.' This was what he had dreaded all these years: another man's child.

'I can't,' Teresa answered simply.

'If you won't give him away then I will,' Marco replied, as if ending the argument.

'No,' she said.

'He can't stay,' Marco reiterated.

'Look at him.'

'I can't,' said Marco firmly. 'I won't.'

'Please,' Teresa begged. 'Look.'

Marco raised his eyes and studied the child. How could he be a father to someone so unlike himself? He tried to reason. 'Can't you see the disgrace?'

Teresa looked down at the child, and then directly into her husband's eyes. 'People will forgive us.'

'They won't,' Marco asserted. 'They'll think you a whore.'

'They know that I was never pregnant. They have seen me. Why else am I called barren?'

'Then they'll think it mine, that I have been with another.'

'I don't care.' Teresa was suddenly fierce again, determined. 'If you loved me then you would love the child.'

'You know that I love you. But how can I love a child that is not mine? Do not ask me to do this. Have I not done enough for you? Cared for you? Loved you?'

'But can't you see?'

'Please . . .' Marco reasoned.

'No. I ask you. I beg you,' his wife replied. 'I will do everything. You don't have to talk to him. You don't even have to look at him if you don't want to. Just let me be with him.'

'Rather than with me.'

'It is not a choice between you and the child.'

'It seems that it is.'

'No,' said Teresa once more. She realised, for the first time, that she liked the sound of the word: its percussive defiance. 'He can work for you. We will need an apprentice.'

'Don't think of such things.'

The child began to wake and cry.

'You see?' said Marco.

'I will care for him. You need do nothing. I will keep him away from you. Nothing about him need concern you.'

Teresa took the boy to the back of the house and fed him the bread softened in milk that she had prepared. She would hide him in the house for the night, stay with him, and protect him against her husband.

She laid the baby on a small upturned wooden bench that she had lined and covered in blankets. He would be safe with her. She would remain with him all night. Perhaps she would never sleep soundly again. Her life was guarding this child: against her husband and against the world.

'Paolo,' she said quietly. 'I will call you Paolo.'

ನಲ

When Teresa woke she knew that something was wrong.

Her son had disappeared.

This was the punishment for all the elation he had given her. She could hear the men downstairs, laughing as they began their day's work. She must ask them, force them even, to tell her what had happened.

'Where's Marco?' she asked the *stizzador*, as he stoked the furnace.

The man shrugged.

'Have you seen the child?' she asked the apprentice.

'The bastard?'

'Not the bastard. The child.'

She felt the fury rise inside her. This was how they spoke. Already the apprentice had learned.

'The foundling.' It was as if he was correcting her.

'My *child*,' she shouted.

For a moment there was silence. The two men turned away.

Teresa walked outside and looked down the street. It started to rain, sudden and hard, momentarily confusing her. She tried to think how far Marco's anger could stretch and the panic made her wild. She ran through the streets, asking all who would listen. She asked the boat builders, vintners, bakers, and butchers; the masons, shoemakers, coopers, and carpenters; the smiths, the fishermen, the barber, and the surgeon if they had seen either her husband or her child. She asked children and grandmothers, the lame and the sick, but it was as if the whole island was locked in a conspiracy to prevent her discovering the truth. Eliana the soothsayer who had never found a husband, Felicia the lace-maker from Burano who had married badly, Franco the blacksmith, Sandro the cooper, Domenico the farrier, Francesco the merchant, Gianni the vintner, Filippo the usurer, even Simona, whom half the island pitied and the other half envied because she too was barren, could not help Teresa in her search.

The rain caught in her hair and splashed up her bare legs. There was nowhere else to go, no one she could ask. Then she thought to check their boat. How could she have been so slow? Was this not the first thing she should have done?

Her sandals were waterlogged and she stopped to take them off, running barefoot through the slippery streets. Perhaps Paolo would be resting in the boat, waiting for her as he had when she had first found him.

She was struck by the shock of memory.

Her pace began to slow, as if she dared not face the inevitability of absence. How could Marco have done this?

She stopped, breathed in, and let the rain fall.

She closed her eyes, praying the boat would be there, and that her husband would be with the child.

But the *sandolo* was gone.

Perhaps she had not prayed hard enough.

Teresa knew that she should go to the church of San Donato and pray without ceasing. She would let God know how much she loved her son.

It was raining so hard that she could hardly see. Her body twitched as she ran, as if shaking off the rain and ridding herself of anxiety were one and the same.

She entered the church, took from the stoop of holy water, genuflected, and ran to the front of the nave.

She slid down onto her knees, and lay prostrate before the altar.

'Mary, Mother of God, Mother of all Mothers, aid me in my distress.

'Mary, Mother of God, Mother of all Mothers, who knows what it is to love a son, aid me in my distress.

'Mary, Mother of God, Mother of all Mothers,
who knows what it is to lose a son, aid me in my
distress.'

She stretched out her arms in submission.

Teresa would not move until Paolo was returned to her. She would lie through every service, each day and every night until Marco, God, and the island had mercy upon her.

For the first hour, no one took any notice. Acts of devotion were common, and the priest almost applauded her piety. But as the day wore on, and services continued, people began to whisper that it was strange she had not moved. One woman noticed that a glass bead from Teresa's rosary had shattered on the floor. Another wondered if she might be dead.

By the afternoon, an elderly lady remarked that she had never seen such piety; another observed that the prostrate woman must have many sins to forgive. At last someone suggested that they should go and tell her husband.

The priest was summoned, and he agreed to fetch Marco himself. It was a husband's job to look after a lunatic wife, not a priest's.

By the time he returned, a crowd of people had congregated under the mosaic of San Donato.

Teresa's head rested in a circle of porphyry that made it look, to the disapproving, as if it had already spilled its blood. To the faithful it could have been a halo.

Then Marco arrived, pushing through the crowd.

He stopped, halfway up the nave.

'Rise, woman.'

Teresa did not move.

'I said, rise.'

Marco looked to the priest, who gestured that he move forward, encouraging him to join her on the floor. Marco was suspicious.

The priest gestured again.

Reluctantly Marco walked forward, stopped, and then crouched down beside his wife, his knees cracking in the echoing church.

Teresa shut her eyes more tightly.

Marco lay down beside her. The cool of the floor began to chill his bones.

'The child is safe,' he said at last.

Still Teresa said nothing.

'Safe,' Marco repeated.

What was he supposed to do?

'He is with the friars, on the Island of the Two Vines. They will look after him.'

Teresa sensed the people were there, watching, but she knew that she had to stay here, completely prostrate, until her husband consented to her every demand. If she capitulated now she would never see Paolo again.

'Only I can look after him . . .'

Marco lay on the floor without knowing what he should do. He listened to his wife breathing as he did when he could not sleep; and, in the cold drama of that moment, he realised that perhaps he had never loved Teresa so much as he did now. She was prepared to humiliate herself or even die to fight for that child. He started to sit up and tried to take her hand, but it lay outstretched, palm down against the marble. 'I am sorry.'

'Give me my son.'

Marco tried to pull Teresa up from the floor, but still she would not move. About to let go, convinced that his wife would do nothing until he brought the child into the church and placed him back in her arms, he replied with two words: 'Our son.'

Teresa's grip tightened. Her left arm bent at the elbow, as if she was beginning to raise her body. She moved slowly, testing her ability to do so, checking that this was no dream. She rose from the ground and put her arms around her husband.

'Let me go there. Let me bring Paolo home.'

'Forgive me,' cried Marco.

Teresa held him to her. 'I will never ask anything of you again.'

The people under the mosaic began to move away. Marco and Teresa were embracing, clothing each other against all the doubts and fears of their future.

೧೮

The next day Teresa rowed across the lagoon to collect her son. She could see the Island of the Two Vines from Murano, the bell tower jutting out amidst the cypress trees, and kept it in her sights throughout the journey, fearing it might disappear if ever she looked away.

She tied up the boat and walked across the marshes. Gradually the ground became firmer. A group of finches started up from the grass as she walked, and the air was loud with the sound of swifts, swallows, and cicadas. Ahead lay a grove of olives.

Teresa stopped.

Underneath the trees lay six open coffins, each one containing a friar.

Perhaps the island was diseased, and the midges and flies of the wasteland had carried an infection in the air. Had Marco lied and sent her here to die? Was the island deserted? And where was Paolo?

Suddenly, one of the dead friars sat up in his coffin and sang.

'Praised be my Lord for our sister the moon, and for the stars, the which he has set clear and lovely in heaven.'

Teresa screamed.

A second dead monk sat up.

'Praised be my Lord for our brother the wind, and for air and clouds, calms and all weather by which thou upholdest life in all creatures.'

Teresa found herself in the middle of a mighty Resurrection, as if Judgment Day had arrived without warning. Each of the monks sat up in turn, arms outstretched, gazing high into the heavens.

'Praised be my Lord for our sister water, who is very serviceable unto us and humble, and precious, and clean.'

'Praised be my Lord for our brother fire, through whom thou givest us light in the darkness; and he is bright and pleasant and strong.'

'Praised be my Lord for our mother the earth, the which doth sustain us and keep us, and bringeth forth divers fruits and flowers of many colours, and grass.'

'Praise ye and bless the Lord, and give thanks unto him, and serve him with great humility.'

The first monk stepped out of his tomb and walked towards her, looking down at the ground as he did so.

'Pax et bonum, peace and all good things, sister . . .'

'My child . . .' Teresa stuttered.

'Our daily orisons . . .' the nearest monk explained, also abandoning his tomb.

'I am Brother Matteo and that is Brother Filippo.' He gestured to the first monk.

The remainder now rose from their coffins but none would look her in the eye. Teresa thought they might be blind.

'Also Brother Giuseppe, Brother Giovanni, Brother Jacopo, and Brother Gentile.'

'I am Teresa, wife of Marco Fiolaro.'

'Then you are blessed,' said Matteo, looking at a patch of ground beneath her feet.

Further silence followed, and the monks stood smiling at the ground as if nothing else need happen.

At last Brother Matteo offered an explanation. 'We rest to prepare ourselves for the eternal slumber, as our brother Francis did before us.'

'My child – my husband brought the child . . .' Teresa stammered.

'He is yours?'

'I know that he came yesterday and that he needs me. He needs me to feed him.'

'We have provided for him. The milk from Sister Goat, the honey from Brother Bee.'

'Where is he?' Teresa asked, desperately trying to encourage them to move, but the monks stood smiling and waiting. Perhaps this was their attempt at eternal life, Teresa reflected. There was no hurry to do anything.

'I think the child is in the library,' Matteo affirmed, and the monks all began to speak at once, as if performing a distracted commentary.

'With Brother Cristoforo.'

'He is old.'

'He has rested much in the afternoon.'

'Time enough in the next world,' added Giovanni.

'And yet he is prepared for greater glory.'

'Sister Death, the Gate of Life.'

Teresa wondered if they were all about to lie down again, as if this encounter had been enough for one day. Perhaps they were waiting for her to do something, or there was some rite of which she was unaware.

'Would you like to see Brother Cristoforo?' Matteo asked.

'He has my son?'

'We have entrusted him to Cristoforo.'

'Can I see him? Can I take my baby home?'

'Rest here a while. Stay with us and pray.'

Teresa's determination gave her strength to resist. 'I must see Paolo.'

'Then follow me.'

They walked up through the olive grove and into the cloisters. Brother Matteo pointed to a step ahead as if warning Teresa not to trip.

'Be mindful . . .'

Teresa looked down.

'Brother Ant.' A small colony was making its way across the step and the monks waited to let it pass.

At last they reached the door of the library. Matteo pushed it open, and Teresa could see an elderly monk reading, holding a piece of quartz shaped like the lesser segment of a sphere midway between his eyes and a manuscript. At his feet sat a small wooden makeshift cradle. The monk looked up.

'My child . . . ?' she asked.

'You are the mother,' the monk asserted. There was no sense of a question; it was a matter of fact.

'I am, Father.'

'Brother,' the monk corrected her.

He knelt down and picked up the baby. 'So short a stay, so happy a child.'

He handed Paolo to Teresa. 'God grant that you take care, sister.'

Teresa held him, and the surge of love returned. 'Paolo,' she said quietly.

Teresa looked up to see all the fellow monks standing in the doorway, their eyes averted. She turned back to Brother Cristoforo.

'Are they blind?' she asked.

The old monk laughed. 'No, not blind. They see very well. But their eyes are fixed on the earth and on the heavens.'

'Why won't they look at me?'

'Our brother Francis scarce knew the features of any woman. He was fearful of his body, Brother Ass. I am too old for temptation, but my brothers' – he smiled – 'do not want to rekindle the spark of vanquished flesh.'

'They are afraid of me . . .'

'Not of you, but of temptation.'

'I am just a mother.' Teresa almost laughed. 'I am too old for that. I am nearly thirty.'

'We have learned to be careful,' said the monk severely. 'A man never knows when the lure of flesh might prove unconquerable.'

'I do not think I pose such a danger.'

The monk waved her away. 'Lady, do not test us. Let us serve the Lord and save our souls.'

'I can go?'

'Take your child, and give thanks.' Then he made the sign of peace and gave her the blessing of St Francis. *'Let him walk in the way of the Lord.'*

MURANO

It was a childhood of swamp and fire.

Almost as soon as he could walk, Paolo was apprenticed to the family glassworks, gathering seaweed and samphire on the shores of the island. He collected pebbles for silica in the marshes as his mother cut branches of elm, alder, and willow for fuel.

The furnace burned night and day from November to July. Marco worked bare-chested, blowing and twisting the glass from his bench. Paolo marvelled at the way in which the thick vitreous paste could purify in the flames to become lucid and brilliant. He let his fingers run through the infinitely varied sharpness of the sand, testing its coarseness and consistency. He examined each constituent part, amazed by the softness of the soda, the alchemical quality of red lead, the threat of arsenic. He loved the way in which the glass mixture, the frit, melted and cracked in the heat, becoming as glutinous and foaming as the waters of the lagoon, surging towards him in the furnace, the hottest sea he had ever seen.

As he grew older Paolo would arrange glass by colour, and visit the mosaicists at work in the churches on the island. He helped them break down stone into tesserae, white from Istria, red from Verona, and watched as they laid the pieces as closely together as possible, pushing them into the wet mortar, brushing off the excess, cleaning the colours with the white of an egg. He took orders to his father as the men asked for a pound of deep red, a bag of emerald, a box of purple. He knew the names by heart: dark blues and deep blacks, purples and violets; the greens of olive, emerald, and oglino; yellow, amber, and his favourite orange vermilion, *becco di merlo*, as bright as the beak of a blackbird. He learned to distinguish between tones, laying out different varieties of colour, assessing the difference between those which complement and those which contrast. He put disparate shapes and tones together, seeing how close blue was to black, or how yellow and blue could not only combine to make green but also intensify into red. He placed sections on top of each other, and watched the mosaic makers lay thin strips of colour over glass to create the brilliance of enamel. One day his mother gave him a small blue crystal and he carried it everywhere, holding it up to the light, watching the way in which different angles of view created different streaks of colour. He closed his eyes and tried to remember each hue and tone.

In the foundry by the fondamenta, Marco provided

tesserae in every colour: *azzurro, beretino, lactesino, rosso* and *turchese,* so that there were blue days and green days, white days and black days. He would experiment with imitation jewellery, vases, bottles, and even beads. He took long tubes of glass and ran a fine wire through their centre, working them over the fire, before cutting them into tiny sections so that they emerged as rounded as pearls. When they had cooled he gave them to his wife and son to thread, and together the family created rosaries, bracelets, and necklaces in imitation quartz and pearl.

Paolo would play with Teresa's ring, a sapphire, placing it on each finger, or rolling it along the ground before holding it up against the light. It was the most precious object she owned, given by her mother just before her death, and she watched Paolo as he played. Perhaps, one day, his wife would wear it.

When Paolo was nine years old, Marco let him blow his first piece of glass. The rod felt heavy in his hand and his father was forced to steady him, but Paolo blew so hard that the glass fell straight off the end, glooping down in a bulbous mass onto the floor.

He then learned how to hold the shaping tongs. He was shocked by the delicacy required; how the incandescent mixture at the end of the pipe could change with the slightest of touches. It was important to be patient, to shape, and reshape, add colour, blow, re-melt, and take time. He was amazed when the glass ballooned out like a foreign object, each globule different in colour, form, and texture, and how quickly he had to work if he wanted to control the molten substance before him.

At times, in the heat and haze of the foundry, Paolo found it hard to concentrate on the end of the blowpipe, or even see it clearly. It was too difficult, and his eyes began to smart.

Marco laughed, placing the rod back in the furnace each time Paolo made a mistake, re-melting again and again until his son learned each skill required.

'Anyone would think you were blind,' he teased.

Paolo apologised, embarrassed by his inability to learn quickly. His father always made it look so effortless.

But Teresa had noticed that her son was almost afraid of the glass. Perhaps it was the heat of the flames, the heaviness of the blowpipe, or the fear of disappointing his father. She tried to ask why he was so hesitant in front of the furnace, glass, and rod.

'I am not fast,' Paolo would reply, and Teresa would comfort him, telling him that he was young, that he would learn, and that he need not be afraid of his father.

She took him to church each morning and prayed for his soul every evening, convinced of the daily need to prepare for the Last Judgment. She taught Paolo that everything that took place on earth was part of God's plan. He must understand the pattern that lay behind his life, and learn of the divine purpose that would lead to salvation from death.

At Mass each day, she looked up in terror as the priest explained the torments of hell in comparison to the bliss of everlasting life; the great chasm of despair that lay between those who would be tortured for evermore and those blessed with eternal felicity. The cleric compared the stench of hell with the sweet perfume of paradise, the screech of the damned with the songs of the saved, and warned of the infernal peril awaiting the unrepentant and the doomed.

Teresa was rapt in religious fervour, holding Paolo tightly against her, while Marco sighed each time the priest made a comparison between the furnaces on the island and the eternal fires of hell, as if no one had thought to make such a connection before. If he could withstand the daily heat of his furnace then the fiery pit of his future held little terror.

Marco had never quite shared the faith of his wife. He was prepared to sit quietly by her side and admit that he was not perfect. He was even willing to make his confession in return for the promise of paradise. But he could not believe the miraculous 'proofs' of faith that the priests had told Teresa. He had never been able to accept that St Olga had lived to the age of nine hundred and sixty-nine; that St Hilarion had survived on fifteen figs a day; or that St Andrew Anagni had once resurrected all the roast birds he had been given for dinner.

Yet when Teresa looked at the church in which she worshipped, built to provide a glimpse of heaven on earth, every story and detail had meaning. She would tell Paolo to compare each stone in a mosaic to a human life and to concentrate upon it. He should know that although a fragment might mean nothing when looked at on its own, it was an essential part of the complete picture, the sum of human life, and only made sense when seen with all the others. Such is the way, she believed, that God looks down upon his creation.

Paolo looked at the mosaic and wondered which his stone might be: whether it lay high or low, in shadow or in darkness. At times, in the early morning, when the sun shone through the windows and caught the gold in its glare, he found that he was forced to squint away from the light, so brightly did it shine. And then, in the darkness of the evening, when they went to pray once more, he would have difficulty making out the shape of the stones in the distance, or discerning the pattern they made.

He would rub his eyes in order to see better, and Teresa would ask him what was wrong. Paolo told her it was nothing. He did not want to alarm his mother or anger his father, and so he would return to the church of San Donato on his own and look at each mosaic closely. When Teresa asked him again what he saw he would no longer guess but remember.

Over the next three years his sight continued to decline.

One evening he was returning from collecting alder wood out near the marshes with his mother. Teresa had lost all sense of time and found it strange that the clock on the campanile stated that it was only five in the afternoon. She wondered aloud if it was accurate.

Paolo asked what she meant.

'Look at the clock.'

'Where?'

'On the campanile.'

'I can see the campanile, but I cannot see the clock.'
Teresa stopped.

'What do you mean? You must be able to see it.'

'I cannot.'

'Then what can you see?'

'I don't know. I can see you. The canal. The houses.'

'Can you see the people in the boat? The women washing?'

'Not clearly,' Paolo replied.

'Did you notice that swift swoop away from you?'

'I heard it. I know its call, but in the skies all the birds are as one.'

'You cannot tell a swallow from a hawk?'

'I do not know.'

'How long have your eyes been like this?'

Teresa was suddenly afraid. She knew that Marco would not tolerate a son who could not see as clearly as he did. At the first sign of any weakness he would cast him out to fend for himself, forever dependent on alms, gifts, and the kindness of strangers.

'Can you describe the end of the fondamenta – the man outside our foundry?' she asked, beginning to panic.

'I can, but it is hard. Is that a man or a woman?'

'You cannot tell? The man has a beard.'

'I cannot see it.'

'Then what can you see?'

'Nearby?'

'No, far off.'

'There is a wall, a shrine, and a cross.'

'Can you see the flowers?'

Paolo paused. Were they roses, or lilies?

'Can you?' his mother insisted.

'No.'

'You cannot tell?'

Paolo could not. But he could see that Teresa was afraid. He knew that her eyes had narrowed and that she was angry: and he recognised that, from now on, he would have to be careful of his replies.

'How can we live if you cannot work the glass?' Teresa asked.

'I do not know,' Paolo replied. For the first time he was scared of his own mother.

'We must find eye crystal to make you see,' Teresa announced. 'Come now. Let's go. In the boat.'

'Now? Without father?'

'He must not know. I will get a man to take us over the water to the *merceria*. There are men there who sell lenses that will help you. I only hope we have the money.'

She pulled at his arm and they made their way to the harbour. There they were rowed over to the mainland. Disembarking on the fondamenta, they walked through the narrow lanes of the Castello, where an elderly hunched man was selling glasses from a tray laid out in the corner of a haberdasher's shop.

Teresa picked at the spectacles so frantically that Paolo thought that she would break them.

'Here, try these.' She handed him a pair of twin lenses, joined at the bridge, but without arms.

'Why are you here?' said the pedlar.

'You do not want us to buy your wares?' Teresa replied abruptly.

'Yes. But the boy is too young for such things . . .'

'He cannot see.'

'But these are for old men, scholars, those who read . . .'

Teresa handed Paolo a magnifying glass.

'Is this better?'

'No, it makes things more blurred in the distance.'

Paolo tried lens after lens, spectacle after spectacle, holding them up by the arms, amazed by the way in which vision in the right eye and then the left swam before him. The goods in the shop became strangely enlarged, almost threatening. Strips of metal, ribbons, bows, buckles, lengths of hemp and twine, mirrors and their reflections, all combined, glass on glass, reflected and refracted, lurching up to meet him.

Paolo's head hurt with the confusion. The lenses fought against each other, and he struggled to find focus.

He felt as if he lived inside a cloud.

Each time he picked up a new lens he could sense his mother's desperate expectation.

'Hold it at a distance,' Teresa ordered.

Paolo stretched out his arm and the building across the street suddenly appeared sharp and clear, the windows glinting in the light against pale-pink stone.

'Now it makes things upside-down,' said Paolo. 'I can

see clearly but I would need to hold the lens at arm's length and walk on my hands.'

'It is meant for close work only,' said the pedlar.

'Can you not make such a lens against my eyes, without the world turned round?'

'What is it that you cannot see?'

'The distance.'

'But you can see close?'

'Clearly. If I look at my finger, I can see the whorls of my skin more distinctly than I can through any glass. Yet nothing else is as true. Everything fades.'

'Alas,' said the pedlar. 'These spectacles are for old men, for scholars, to aid in reading. I have nothing for sight such as yours. The glass cannot be made for such a purpose.'

'Then what can we do?' Teresa asked.

'You could visit Luciano the apothecary. He may have a remedy; but he is not always reliable . . .'

'We must go to him now,' said Teresa, pulling Paolo away, 'before your father realises, before anyone knows that you cannot see . . .'

'I can see.'

'Not well enough. Marco will be able to tell. We must prevent him knowing of this.' She called to the pedlar. 'Goodbye.'

They crossed three streets and made their way to the jewellers' quarter. Paolo found the busy alleys more frightening than the objects in the shop. He seemed to be permanently in the way of another person, someone with more pressing business. Crowds pushed past. Horses reared up in front of him. The streets stank of excrement. He longed to be home.

Luciano the apothecary worked in a shop crammed with hanging herbs, pottery jars of powders, liquids, and unguents. He sat behind a curtain of bright flame and bubbling amber liquid. A great mortar with a heavy pestle hung from the ceiling, and majolica jars lined the room, holding saffron, pepper, ginger, cinnamon, clove, nutmeg, cassia, and galinga. Every object in the shop appeared to be black, silver, white, or gold; as if this spectrum of colour held a symbolic secret that only the apothecary could fathom. As soon as they entered his laboratory Luciano began to talk of a new alchemical invention which was nothing less than a recipe for everlasting life. It involved mixing the scales of a fish with powdered gold and the eyelid of a snake, and he was convinced of its efficacy.

Teresa interrupted. 'My son cannot see.'

The apothecary put down his tools. 'He is blind?'

'No, but he cannot tell distance.'

'That is common enough.'

'It may be so, but then he cannot work at my husband's craft.'

Luciano turned to the child. His eyes were sunk deep in his head, as if he himself had trouble with sight. Now he came close, looking hard at Paolo.

'How old are you?'

'I am twelve.'

'Is the light too bright for you?'

'Not here, no.'

'Where? When?'

'In the heat of the day. The brightness . . .'

'Is it too strong?'

'Sometimes it hurts my eyes.'

'I understand. Come. Stand in the doorway.' The apothecary put his arm around Paolo's shoulder.

'Look out into the street now. What do you see?'

'I see shape, not detail. Colour, not form.'

'You live, perhaps, in a clouded world?'

'Sometimes I cannot see the clouds. People tell me they are there, or that a storm is coming, but I am unable to perceive such things. Such forms are like sheets of white across the sky, darkening slowly and then becoming black. I see them move but they are as mists.'

The apothecary told Paolo that sight was a dance of two rays, perpetually changing, between perception and object. The eye was filled with seeing and the object was luminous with colour. Paolo's problem was that his eyes lacked sufficient power.

'Do you eat many onions?' Luciano asked suddenly.

'No,' replied Paolo.

'Of course you eat onions,' said Teresa.

'Yes, but I don't like them.'

'Falconers find their sight improves if they forgo onions. Have you tried balms and ointments?'

Paolo knew nothing of such things. He was silent. Teresa attempted to explain.

'He has sought no cure. The lack of sight is new to him.'

The apothecary sighed, leaned forward, and held up a candle.

'Come here, my child. Look into this light.'

It was held so close and became so bright that Paolo flinched. Luciano came as near as possible, and looked hard into each eye. His breath smelled of tomatoes.

'Let me think,' he said.

'Surely we need a balm,' said Teresa, 'a potion, a tincture, or an ointment? Something we can put on his eyes to make them well.'

Luciano confessed that there were such treatments but he had still to be convinced of their efficacy. He had heard how celandine, fennel, endive, betany, and rue could all help restore eyesight; as well as pimpernel, ewe's milk, red snails, hog's grease, and the powdered head of a bat. Some recommended the application of leeches to the eyelids, and he had learned that a doctor in Padua had recently suggested that those with weaknesses of the optic spirit might gain comfort from hanging the eyes of a cow round their neck. He had studied recipes that involved the venom of toads, the slaver of a mad dog, wolfsbane, aconite tubers, and the burned skin of a tarantula.

After some thought he suggested that he try a balm he had made from mixing eyebright with white wine, distilled until it was ready to drink. Two handfuls of herbs were mixed with hog's grease and beaten with a pestle and mortar. This thick ointment had been left in the sun for three days, boiled, strained, and pressed three times before it was ready to coat the eyes.

Teresa smeared the balm gently over Paolo's eyelids, but it only closed his world still further.

'You must apply it thickly,' advised the apothecary.

Paolo reached out and took a scoop of the lard-like salve. It was dense and greasy, and it made his eyes feel heavy with sleep.

'Now rest,' he heard the man say. 'Rest for two hours.'

Paolo lay down in the darkness. Was this what it might be like to be blind? What would it mean to live in such blackness for ever, never seeing his mother again, reliant on memory alone? He wanted to reach out, cling to her, and then let her wash the darkness away.

'Keep still,' Luciano commanded.

Teresa had begun to pray.

When the time had passed, the apothecary wiped off the paste and asked Paolo what he saw.

'Strange shapes, which I cannot trust. Not lines; only close objects have an outline. Everything else is blurred.'

'Has your sight improved?' Teresa asked.

Paolo desperately wanted to please his mother but found that he could not. He shook his head.

'But what of colour? You see colour clearly?' Luciano asked.

'Close, yes. I know colour.'

'You find it restful?'

'Sometimes.'

'And you know what it can do?'

'What do you mean?'

The apothecary spoke as if he was conveying the secret of life itself. 'Sometimes, when colour appears on the body, it must be met with colour; we must concentrate upon it, wear it, dream it, look at it, and eat it.'

'What do you mean?' asked Teresa.

The apothecary sighed. 'Trouble from the colour red, for example, must be met with red. We must think red thoughts, wear red clothes, and eat red food. It can help to heal burns and blood vessel diseases, bleeding gums and irregular menstruation: all things red. The colour brown is good for hoarseness, deafness, epilepsy, and anal itching; whereas the colour white can aid men with hiccups, belching, and impotence. Think on these things. Fight colour with colour.'

'And does every colour have a purpose?'

'Of course. Purple is good for stuttering, muscle degeneration, and the loss of balance. Yellow can help with nausea, obesity, and gas in the stomach . . .'

'But what do you recommend for my son?'

'I suggest the calming properties of the colour blue.'

'What kind of blue?' asked Paolo.

'All kinds. Azure, hyacinth, peacock, and cornflower. Begin with the water outside, the canals – look into them for four hours each day and your eyes will be rested.' He turned to Teresa. 'Show him a sapphire. Perhaps two. Use your husband's blue glass.'

'And this will cure his sight?' she asked.

'It will help him. But if, for some unlikely reason, this does not work then we will try the colour yellow' – the apothecary paused – 'although you may not find that so agreeable.'

'Why?' asked Teresa.

'The treatment consists of warmed urine, fresh butter, and capon fat. But perhaps that is better than the bile used by Tobias, or the disembowelled frogs so favoured by the Assyrians.'

His mother looked worried. 'You think that you can do this, Paolo?'

'I can try.'

She paid eleven *soldi* for the advice and took Paolo home as the dusk fell.

ഇ

The next day Teresa asked her son to concentrate on the canal outside the foundry. 'Start here and I will try to find some blue glass.'

She kissed him briefly on the forehead and turned away down the street.

Paolo stared into the water. It was dark and cerulescent, flecked by bright white when the light hit it, flashing brilliantly, too intensely for Paolo's eyes in the middle of the day. He sought out sunless areas, under the bridges where the shadow would darken into blue-black. He tried to follow the path of the tide, changing the angles at which he looked, seeking the calmest areas of blue, and the softest light on his eyes.

He wondered at colour: how each one seemed to bleed into another, to combine and then to repel in the changing light, so that after a few days of looking at the water he could no longer describe the way in which it shaded off into aquamarine the further he gazed out to sea.

Then he looked at the seaweed clinging to the stakes and piles, at the vegetation already growing on the marble steps, the weeds springing up on the bridge by the church, and the new green shutters on the houses. He looked up through pine trees towards the sky, but the light was too bright and hurt his eyes, the pine cones appearing like black spots on the surface of his cornea, floating across his vision.

Teresa gave him two pieces of deep-blue glass cut into squares, like large tesserae. He felt the sharpness of their edges, rough in his hand.

'I found them in the workshop. Your father thought I was mad.'

Paolo kept his left eye closed and raised one of the squares to his right eye, so that the bright water softened under the deep-blue glass. Soon he felt strangely calm, stilled by the sights he saw. He looked from sunlight to shade, endlessly intrigued by the way in which the intensity of the light affected the colour of the object he studied.

He began to walk around the island with blue glass held up against his eye. Most of the time this gave him comfort, but when he looked at bright light reflecting off the lagoon, it was as if the glass in front of his eye had shattered. He marvelled at the endless refraction. At times there was such a serene wash of light that there appeared to be no colour at all. At other moments, with the light behind him, or in the shadows of buildings, he could see his own face clearly reflected in the blue glass, though distorted into a strange oval. Paolo began to dream in blue, imagining he lived in an underwater world where he could discern even less than he could on land.

Yet although he could admit to his mother that the world had become calmer, there was no greater clarity, and his distant vision had become worse.

Teresa sat with him by the side of the canal. 'Come. Kneel down.' She scooped water in her hands and began to wash his eyes. Then she dried them with her dress. 'What am I to do with you?' she asked.

Paolo opened his eyes and felt the world swim around him.

'I can see well enough,' he said quietly. 'I can learn to guess.'

'You cannot survive by guessing,' Teresa replied.

She could cover her son's faults in the home, but not by the furnace.

ನಿಲ

The accident made everything clear.

It was late afternoon and the room was filled with smoke, haze, and heat. The blowpipes were re-heating in the furnace in preparation for drawing glass. Paolo was checking that the ends were red-hot.

'Bring one over,' his father had called.

For a moment Paolo was unsure. He knew the layout of the foundry. He had memorised the precise position of each tool and the daily habits of the people who worked there. But in the heat of this particular afternoon he was strangely lost.

'Come on,' Marco shouted.

Paolo turned, blowpipe in hand, and the heated end swung into Marco's bare arm, burning into the flesh. For an instant there was silence, horror: then his father screamed in pain.

'What have you done? Did you not see my arm was there?'

The *stizzador* rushed to fetch water. Paolo dropped the rod and rushed out into the street. His mother, drawn by the cries, ran down from above.

'My God.'

Paolo stayed away for three hours, while his mother bandaged the wound and Marco raged. 'That boy will never be any good. He's slow, he dreams. He couldn't even see where I was.'

'Rest,' said Teresa. 'Don't think about that now.'

'He cannot see. That is the truth. You have been protecting him. You thought I hadn't noticed.'

'I prayed you would not.'

Teresa soaked a fresh piece of cloth in water and applied it to his arm. 'What can we do?'

'Nothing, of course. No one else will take him.'

'He is young,' she said. 'He tries hard. And he is frightened of you.'

'That makes no difference to his affliction. Fear does not make men blind.'

Teresa knew that this was not the time to argue. 'Let him do what he is good at. There are things he can do.'

'What?'

'He loves colour. He concentrates on it. He understands it. Let him prepare and sort the glass. I will help him.'

'You work hard enough for him as it is. How can you do more?'

'Don't be angry with him.'

'We can't have accidents by the furnace. You know that.'

Teresa eased the bandage on his arm, and stroked Marco's hair. 'You have been brave.' She smiled.

'The wound will heal, won't it?' he asked.

'Yes,' she replied. 'It will. Let me bring you some wine.'

Work ceased for the day, and they sat together outside the foundry in the evening light. Teresa never understood how Marco's temper could rise and fall so quickly. 'Can we not love Paolo for what he is?' she asked.

'I try, but I can never forget the boy is not my son. You can love him but I do not know how. He's quiet. He hardly speaks. He doesn't even look like me. He's so hard to love.'

'Then love him for me, for my sake.'

'I do. That is what I do. Can you not see that this is

what I am doing? This is how I live. Only for you. The boy is . . .'

Then Marco stopped. Teresa turned round.

Paolo had returned and was listening.

'How long have you been there?' Marco asked.

Paolo looked at his mother. 'What did he mean – "I can never forget the boy is not my son"?'

Teresa remembered the first word Paolo had ever spoken. *Gone*. Even then she thought that he had been speaking of his natural mother; her absence. He had sensed her fears. And she had vowed then that she would never tell him. Why should he ever know?

'It does not mean I do not love you,' she said simply.

'Teresa . . .' said Marco.

She walked over and tried to comfort Paolo. 'You have been as a son.'

'But you did not give me life. I have another mother.'

His eyes had become accusatory.

'Yes.'

'Where is she?'

'Lost. Unknown.'

'How can this be?'

Marco stood up. 'Teresa rescued you.'

Paolo ignored him, concentrating all his attention on his mother. 'But why didn't you tell me?'

Teresa looked at him. 'I was frightened.'

'Of what?'

'Of this.'

Paolo didn't know whether to feel fury, betrayal, loss,

or sympathy for Teresa's fear. He no longer understood who he was, or his place in the world. What was he, if not their son?

At last Marco spoke.

'No one could love you as your mother has loved you.'

'She is not my mother.'

'She has been as a mother. And you have lived because of her.'

'Perhaps I should have died.'

'No,' said Marco fiercely. 'Don't speak like that. You should learn from her.'

'Learn what?'

'Gratitude.'

'Don't argue,' said Teresa. 'Please. I have done all that I can. I have not lived for myself, but only through you. I wanted to do this. I wanted to love.'

'And I will never know my true mother?'

'No.'

'Did she die in childbirth?'

'We do not know.'

Marco took Paulo to look into the heat of the furnace. 'Teresa has been the truest mother you could ever have wanted. Her love is fierce, as strong as this flame. Do not ever doubt her.'

Paolo tried to think who his real mother might have been, and what he had inherited from her: perhaps the weakness in the eyes, the way he walked, or the manner in which he held his head when he listened.

What must she have been like? Was she ill or poor?

Was he conceived out of love or out of desperation, lust, or violence? How was he born? And who was his father?

Why could he never know?

And how could they have carried such a secret for so long?

ॐ

As their work continued in the foundry Marco tried hard to tolerate Paolo's mistakes as if he were one of the slower apprentices. He made allowances for his poor sight, letting him work closely with the glass, keeping him clear of the blowpipes and the flames. Paolo mixed vegetable soda ash, silica sand, and ground quartz pebbles; he prepared glass pastes and gold-leaf tesserae; he added colour by stirring up solutions of manganese, iron, and copper filings to produce deep violets, pale yellow, rich green, and dark amber; and he checked the opacity and the lustre of each piece they produced.

He raised the samples close against his eyes, and then held them at varying distances, watching the way in which they changed in the light, surprised by translucence, amazed by clarity. He passed into a reverie of fascination whatever he held, whether it was a piece of glass, a tessera, a goblet, or a bowl. Each object only had meaning for him when it was closely observed.

On the feast of the Assumption, in the year thirteen hundred and eleven, Paolo was asked to show Simone, a painter from Siena, all the glass and tesserae they possessed, for he wanted to use them as imitation jewels, studding the golden haloes of the saints, in his next altarpiece.

Although the painter was only twenty-six years old it was clear that he was already a successful man. He seemed almost careless of life and possessed all the confidence gained by a good apprenticeship, inherited wealth, and appreciated talent. His expensive clothes were worn nonchalantly, as if he was unaware of their worth, and the blue-and-white cap on his head looked like a half-unravelled turban which could fall off at any moment.

Paolo carried the glass outside, bringing blue sapphires, gold-red rubies, green emeralds into the bright daylight.

'These are good,' said Simone. He examined each piece carefully but then appeared distracted, as if Paolo was standing too close to him, blocking his light. 'You look very pale,' he observed. 'Do your parents never let you outside?'

'In the summer the sun is so bright that it hurts my eyes,' said Paolo, 'and so I try to find shadow. I have always been fair.'

'Extraordinary. You are as pale as a town egg. Perhaps I should paint you. I am always using the people I meet in my work. You cannot imagine how many Venetian merchants I've expelled from the Temple.'

Paolo was curious and suddenly amused. 'Who would I be?'

The painter examined him once more, looking at the way the light fell on his face. 'You are rather beautiful.

Such strange blue eyes. You could be an angel. Or the magician Elymas struck blind by Paul. If you grew your hair, you could even be a girl. St Lucy, perhaps, the saint who plucked out her eyes because her lover would not cease from praising her beauty.' He picked out a yellow stone. 'Do you know that she was drowned in a vat of boiling urine? Not very pleasant.'

They walked back into the foundry and Paolo took Simone to the storeroom. Here he displayed each piece of glass in different lights, showing the painter how it changed from sunlight to shadow. Then he asked on which wall the painting would be situated: whether north or south, east or west, and if there would be windows close by.

He held glass up against the window and in the doorway, asking Simone at which time of day the light would fall on his painting and for how long? Did it move from right to left or from left to right? Had he seen the mosaics in the church of San Donato?

Paolo was so serious in his questioning that for the first time that afternoon Simone was silenced and thoughtful.

'I always follow the dominant light,' he replied at last.

Paolo asked what colours the painter would be using, and how much gold leaf he could extract from a florin. If the Virgin's cloak was to be blue then which particular blue might it be: cobalt, azurite, or indigo? Perhaps a glass amethyst might work as a clasp, but would he like it to be cut in any special way, faceted or made round?

The painter smiled. 'How do you know such things?' he asked.

Marco had entered the storeroom and was listening. 'His eyes are not as others'.'

Simone turned to Marco. 'He has extraordinary ability. He speaks of light and colour as if they were his greatest friends.'

'They are all he knows.'

'Are you happy here?' The painter turned to Paolo.

'Of course he is happy,' Marco interrupted. 'Why might he not be?'

'I was only thinking.'

'What?' asked Paolo.

'If you would like to come and work for me.'

'Where?'

'In Siena, of course.' Simone turned to Marco. 'Let me take him for a year. I will train him. He can cut and set the glass in my work.'

'And you would pay him?'

'Enough to live, of course,' said Simone. 'I am not a tyrant. I have work both in my own town and in Assisi. The life of St Martin. Windows and walls. It will be an adventure.'

Paolo could not quite believe what Simone had said.

'Well?' asked the painter. 'You know stone and you know glass. If you really want to understand colour then you must also make paint. Grind it from the stone, gather it from the earth; coax it, blend it, mix it. The darkest indigo. The deepest alizarin. Infinite blue. There is nothing more exciting than letting colour reveal itself.'

It was the first time Paolo had been offered control of his destiny. 'Can I choose?' he asked Marco.

His father nodded.

'Decide,' the painter continued. 'I will teach you. Together we will create a new earth and a new heaven.'

It would mean leaving all that he had known: the end of childhood.

'I will come,' said Paolo.

'What will your mother say?' asked Simone.

'I think we should keep it from her,' Marco answered. 'She will not agree.'

Paolo tried to imagine the farewell. 'If I have to say goodbye to her then I will never leave.'

'So it is agreed. Not a word to your mother. Let us set out tomorrow,' announced Simone. 'Your life as an apprentice begins.'

ജ

As Marco had predicted, Teresa was furious. 'What have you done, agreeing to such a thing?' she railed.

'It is the boy's choice, not mine. I did not even suggest it.'

'I don't believe you. Paolo would not leave me in such a way.'

'He has found employment, adventure. He may make us rich yet.'

'If we live to see the day.'

'It is only a year.'

'Every day will seem a year. I will not know where he is or what he is doing, if he is happy or sad, hungry or thirsty, healthy or well. I will not know if he sleeps or no; nor will I be able to comfort him when he is anxious. You have to be a mother to know what it is when a son leaves.'

'And you have to be a father to know when a boy is no longer a child. He is sixteen years old. He should be employed, married, away from us both.'

'He is employed.'

'Only because you do half his work.'

'That is not true.'

'You know that it is.'

Teresa left the house and walked along the fondamenta, past the church of Santo Stefano, and over the bridge towards the church of San Donato. She only stopped when she came to the edge of the island and looked out to sea, towards the Island of the Two Vines. There was a haze over the water. Everything seemed distant, blurred. This must be what it has always been like for Paolo, she thought.

She remembered finding him in the little *rio* on Ascension Day, the rescue from the monks and his work in the foundry; his strange blue eyes, and the way he looked at her as if he could never quite believe what he was seeing. It was a look of both trust and bewilderment. Only she knew it, as if such a look was meant only for her.

Who would look after him now?

As she walked by the shoreline and thought of her son, Teresa became convinced that her passionate concern was Paolo's only protection.

She began to imagine every possible illness or accident that might befall him, because if she did so then perhaps such disasters might never happen.

Her head filled with all the ways in which her son might die.

SIENA

It was August. Simone planned to journey south through Padua, Ferrara, and Bologna, over the foothills of the Apennines and then cross the River Arno to the east of Florence. They rode in the back of a cart through winding paths amidst sloping vineyards, collecting water from the wells of the small hill towns which studded their route. After eight days Paolo could just make out the silhouette of the city of Siena high in the distance, a huddle of ochre and deep brown, its buildings folding into each other, framed by crenellations of cypress and pine.

Simone's workshop lay in the Contrada Aquila. It was situated in a spacious courtyard that opened beside a crowded narrow street. Here the apprentices were trained how to prepare the wood for devotional panels and altar-pieces: washing, smoothing, and rubbing down each piece of poplar before applying the foundation of gesso. The more experienced amongst them worked on ornamentation: pressing tin and gold leaf, beginning to gild, burnish, pounce, punch, and stamp. Others employed on frescoes outside the workshop had already learned how to mark up a wall, to wet it down, plaster, true up, and smooth off.

Simone told Paolo that he must know every part of the process of painting: preparing charcoal for drawing, making brushes, paper, and pens, and collecting eggs with which to bind pigment and make the paint tempera mixture. He had to sift lime and sand, prepare plaster, smooth panels, and then, at last, when he fully understood the process, he would be allowed to work with colour.

'What are you painting?' asked Paolo.

'Everything,' replied Simone. 'Alpha and Omega. The beginning and the end.'

'You are painting heaven?'

'And hell. Out of this humble earth. Can you believe it?' The artist spoke like a showman addressing an audience. 'I select each ingredient, like a wife at the market. I cook with paint.' He crumbled a piece of ochre between his thumb and forefinger. 'As a chef coaxes flavour so I encourage colour: with egg and tempera, red madder, and saffron. These are my ingredients and my spices.' He flicked the paint away. 'There is only one difference.'

'And what is that?'

'The meal I create is everlasting.'

Simone was happiest when he had an audience, and Paolo began to wonder if his apprentices were employed not only to undertake the menial tasks which their master had outgrown, but also to provide constant attention, ever ready to laugh at his wit. Keeping Simone amused was almost half of the work because he could be plunged into depression at any moment, such was the fragility of his confidence and, Paolo noticed, his fondness for wine. The man could move from exhilaration to despair in an instant, which made all those who worked for him both nervous and watchful.

At times Simone would throw down his brush, leaving the workshop to drink with his friends, returning too inebriated to continue. He would then compensate for such wildness by working without stopping for thirty-six hours. Talented, unpredictable, and easily distracted, he sometimes gave his pupils astonishing bursts of responsibility.

'Lippo, do the hands – Mino, finish this halo – Ugolino, decorate the cloak of the Virgin.'

'How?'

'Make it up!'

Paolo began by preparing charcoal for drawing: taking strands of willow and cutting them into matchsticks, smoothing and sharpening them like spindles, tying them in bunches, and then placing them in an earthenware pot which he took each night to the baker's, letting the strands roast until morning.

After four months he learned how to work with colour, grinding pigment from stone on slabs of porphyry or serpentine. In order to make azure, he would boil up hot alkaline mixtures of honey and lye in a series of bowls and then add the pigment, keeping a close eye as the colour gradually settled. Once he had drawn off the liquid, he would be left with paint ready to bind with egg yolk and apply to either panel or fresco.

Just as he had learned to define each shade of stone and glass, so Paolo now began to see how paint could lighten or darken, enrich, or become dull in a moment.

'Our task is nothing less than to show the glory of God's creation. Painting is an act of faith, Paolo. We tell stories, inspire devotion. This is the land of miracles' – Simone smiled – 'even if they sometimes become repetitive.'

'What do you mean?'

'Saints can be tedious, do you not think? There are only so many ways in which a painter can depict devotion. Hell is so much more diverting.' As they blended pigment with egg yolks, Simone began to tell Paolo of his ambition to paint a Last Judgment: the dead emerging from the cracks and fissures of the earth, skeletal, ghostly, waiting either to be clothed in flesh or tormented in hell, haunted by a pale blue light. As he warmed to his theme the story became filled with dreadful detail. There would be blazing rivers and bottomless pits of volcanic despair containing the stained souls of the damned, blackened by sin and lit with flames. Usurers would have to swallow hot coins, and sodomites would be skewered like pigs. Slanderers with their mouths stretched and cut open would be seen with their teeth ground to a pulp and then re-grown only to be pulverised once more. The painting should be a vision of eternal misery, and above it all would be Satan with three bastard heads, bat's wings, and Judas hanging, half-eaten, from his mouth.

'So you can see that painting heaven is somewhat dull after all that,' Simone concluded. 'We need drama, not everlasting felicity. But this, of course, is our challenge. To make paradise exciting. A place beyond belief.'

తుం

Although he was a craftsman by day Simone was something of a dandy by night, wearing a different tunic for each evening's *passeggiata*, but cut in the same style, and always in velvet: maroon on a Monday, azure on a Tuesday, vermilion on a Wednesday, burnt gold on a Thursday, lamp black on a Friday, crimson on a Saturday, and white on a Sunday. He rubbed his gums with mint, shaved, washed, and then scented himself with rosewater. Before he left the workshop he checked his appearance in a silvered mirror, and adjusted his curling hair accordingly. Life was a performance and he was its leading actor, presenting and perfuming himself before the world.

The true test of his showmanship came when the Commune of the City announced a competition to paint a fresco of the Coronation of the Virgin, a Maestà, for the Palazzo Pubblico. All the painters of the city were invited to compete: Segna di Buonaventura, Memmo di

Filippuccio, Dietisalvi, and Simone. This was the first great secular commission, and it would rival Duccio's golden Maestà in the cathedral, filling the east wall of the town hall.

Simone was determined to win and set to work immediately, laying out sketches of saints and angels, martyrs, apostles, and church fathers. He began to experiment with azurite and malachite, and brought in great swathes of fabric on which he could base his design for the Virgin's mantle. Two assistants were asked to find new ways of gilding metal, so that the haloes of the saints would glow under candlelight as evening fell.

'This is not only painting,' he cried; 'we must be the envy of all other trades: the goldsmiths, the weavers, and the dressmakers. We must paint what cannot be achieved on earth. That is our secret. We will depict the impossible.'

Paolo was asked to make charcoal for the preparatory drawings – the Virgin as Mother of God and Queen of Heaven, holding the Christ child, with the four patron saints of the city kneeling below: Ansanus, Savinus, Crescentius, and Victor.

'Hold still,' cried Simone. 'You make a perfect saint. Keep working.'

As Paolo bound each twig of willow, Simone began to draw him. The pale face and blond hair curling under the ears. The thin nose. Long fingers. And Paolo's strangely quiet blue eyes, endlessly puzzled, curious, surprised.

'Which saint am I?'

'Ansanus, the young Roman nobleman who first baptised the Sienese. Try to look more spiritual.'

'I don't feel very spiritual.'

'Then look serene.'

'Can't I just be myself?'

'No, no, that is not the point at all. Have you not listened to anything I have said? We must turn men into angels and make the heavens sing. Colour and joy. We are painting infinity,' Simone cried.

తిం

Over three hundred councillors assembled to discuss the commission. Each painter had been asked to present his ideas in the council chamber where the Signori of the Nine, and the Consiglio della Campana gathered around their drawings. One painter suggested a celebratory painting of the recent acquisition of Talamone and a glorious gallery of all lands recently conquered. Another put forward his plan for an enormous panel of the Battle of Montaperti and the conquest of Montalcino; while a third proposed a representation of the day Buonaguida Lucari had laid the keys of the city on the altar of the cathedral and donated all that they had to the mercy of the Virgin Mary, their protectress against the iniquitous and evil Florentines.

As his rivals struggled to make their case, Simone was both impatient and exhilarated, for he was convinced that none could match his vision of divine beneficence.

'This is my plan,' he announced. 'The Court of Heaven and the Seat of Good Government presiding over us all. I will paint the other, eternal world: things unseen and unimagined. The fresco will be a banner from heaven and a blessing on earth, containing all riches. Wisdom. Stillness. Calm. I will show you wonders.'

He walked over to the windows. 'As the light from the south wall forever changes, so will this painting. Each time you look you will discover truth. The Virgin will sit high above us in an exquisitely embroidered mantle, a garment so rich and so beautiful that it will make the textile workers weep to see it. Her throne will echo that which sits below in the council chamber, and her seat will be our inspiration for both justice and mercy. She will offer us the Christ child, our salvation from death, our guide to the divine and our Redeemer. The scroll held by the child will be of paper, the text of ink. *Love justice, you who love the earth*. The Book of Wisdom.

'Everything about this Maestà will reflect the majesty of maternal love. There will be jewels in the clothing of the Madonna and diamonds in the tracery of the windows behind her. In the distance the sky will darken into an infinite blue without limit, for there is no end to the glory of paradise. I will turn pigments from the earth, real earth, into heaven.'

Simone made a low bow.

'I offer you stillness, joy, and peace. My painting will depict our gift from God, the everlasting bounty of heaven, and the grace of our salvation. I have seen this beauty. Only let me paint it for you, here in this room, a divine blessing on our fair and noble city.'

The councillors were silent. The commission was won.

 හ

By the time Simone returned home to the workshop he was drunk.

'Victory,' he cried. 'Victory by St Victor. This is a noble day. We have routed our enemies and made straight the high road to our salvation. The whole town attests to my brilliance.'

At first his apprentices were almost frightened by such exuberance, unable to understand quite what their master was saying.

'I will smooth plaster with the thighbone of a gelded lamb. I will burnish each halo with sapphire. We shall prosper, and we shall vanquish all. *Salute! Salute! Grandi amici!'*

More wine was opened, and Simone began to elaborate on his performance, telling all who would listen of his plan to create eternity in paint.

'The divine stillness, this is what I have promised, the life of the spirit on this earth. A foretaste of heaven.'

'And how will we do this?' asked Paolo.

Simone seemed oddly reluctant to answer.

'By genius and hard work, of course,' he replied testily.

But Paolo could see that Simone was looking at him strangely, as if he had suddenly remembered something important.

'What is it?' he asked when they were alone.

Simone looked embarrassed. 'There is something I must confess to you, now that we have secured the commission.'

'Ah,' said Paolo.

'When I was talking to the Consiglio I told them a story.'

There was something about Simone's apologetic tone that made Paolo uneasy.

'What was it?'

'It was of a man who had recently been a prisoner in Genoa.'

'I have heard the apprentices talk of such a person. The man of a million lies.'

'Exactly. Only this time I think he was telling the truth.'

'Continue.'

'He had travelled the world for many years, and he had seen the most miraculous sights. He had been to Persia, Cathay, and the Indies. He had seen golden men. Wondrous palaces. Horses descended from Bucephalus. Flocks of cranes filling the sky. But when I asked him to tell me the greatest of the wonders, he stopped, as if no one had asked him such a question before. He spoke quickly and secretively; telling of a mountain hidden away on the edge of the world which contained the most perfect blue stone. It was lapis lazuli, the truest blue he had ever seen, and it seemed that the colour would last for all eternity.

'I asked him if he thought a man could make paint

from such a stone, and he told me that if such a thing were possible then it would be as if a man were painting the dome of heaven, so precious and perfect was that colour.

'This is what I told the Consiglio. That, from the moment I heard this story, I have been determined to acquire that blue. And I will do so. It will be the glory of the city.'

'But how can we find such a colour?'

'It has to be gathered from the ends of the earth.'

'And how will we do that?'

'This is the awkward moment.'

'Go on.'

'I told them that you would go.'

'What?'

'Clearly I cannot go myself, because I will be painting; but you, who know, love, and understand colour ... think of the joy of such a discovery. A blue that is not fugitive or transitory but permanent and eternal.'

'But I can hardly see my way out of the door. How could I ever make such a journey?'

'I will give you a guide.'

'That's no use.'

'He's very reliable.'

'Who is he?'

'Jacopo, a jewel merchant. He's Venetian like you. I am sure that you will find his company agreeable.'

Paolo was so taken aback that he could only continue the argument. 'And why is he going?'

'Because he is obsessed with jade and is determined to go to Cathay to find it. The mountain is almost on the way. In Badakhshan.'

'But it will be thousands of miles.'

'Think of the adventure. How few will have made such a journey.'

'And how few have survived. You are mad.'

'Jacopo is keen. I told him you had the most extraordinary gift for colour.'

'How kind of you.'

'You should be grateful. Such an adventure.'

'You go then.'

'Alas, my talent must remain here.'

'And how long did you say the painting would take?'

'About a year.'

'But that is too short.'

Simone reached for more wine. 'Don't worry about deadlines. It only encourages them.'

Paolo could not believe Simone's nerve. 'Let me understand. You have promised that Jacopo and I will travel to the ends of the earth in search of a colour we do not know exists and return within a year?'

'Or two. It doesn't matter too much as long as you do, indeed, return.'

'And what if I say no?'

'You won't. You love me. You love colour. It will make your fortune. And then, in paint, we will enter time itself. The blue will let us penetrate the mystery and understand the nature of God's creation, our infinite and eternal future. By seeing this perfect blue we will be given a glimpse of everlasting life.'

'But what if Jacopo will not take me?'

'He will. You will be his Sabbath Gentile.'

'And what is that?'

'I can never remember how it works. You carry things on holy days because they can't. Something like that. So Saturdays are busy. He is coming to eat with us this evening.'

'But how will I live?'

'I will give you some money. And then you must do what the *verixelli* do. Take our glass and trade it as stone. A few real sapphires amidst the glass and you could do well.' Simone appeared to have thought of everything.

'I would have to lie.'

'You have already learned to lie about your sight. It would not be such a big untruth; all merchants exaggerate the worth of their wares.'

'And if I fail?'

'You won't fail. I have seen how obsessed you can be. Think what such a discovery might mean. You wanted excitement in your life. I have given it to you. How else were we supposed to win the commission?'

ॐ

That night, a small Jewish man arrived at the workshop. He must have been fifty years old, for his beard had greyed, and his back had already begun to show the stoop of age. A yellow circle was fixed to his hat.

'Jacopo,' cried Simone, 'my friend. The man who knows the way.'

'I am foolish coming here,' the old man murmured, 'and I do so only as a favour to your uncle.'

'On the contrary,' said Simone, 'it is you who are being given the blessing.'

'I have heard that you have a boy who might help me on my travels. Is this the one?'

Simone nodded.

Jacopo looked at Paolo as if he were buying a slave in the market, assessing his size, weight, and strength. 'I am told that you have a keen eye.'

'I can tell stone for stone and glass for glass.'

'Then let us begin.'

'Already?' asked Paolo.

'Why not?' Jacopo reached into his pocket and pulled out a velvet pouch from which he removed four stones. 'Three of these are false: glass. One is true. Tell me which is which.'

Paolo started with a sapphire.

'This is not real.'

'And how would you know?'

'It is too clear. A sapphire is like the darkest sea . . .'

'Go on . . .'

'Held up to the light, it changes. The flaws refract. This stone is too good. It needs imperfections, uncertainty. If you mean to deceive, a glass should have a flaw.'

'When did you last see a sapphire?' Jacopo asked.

'When I was a child. My mother had a ring.'

'You can remember?'

'I know the blue of stone and the blue of glass.'

Now Paolo held a ruby up to the light. He brought it close to his eye and then moved it away again, at a distance.

'Like blood,' he said.

'What kind of blood?'

'New sprung.'

'The great Tartar Emperor once said that he would give a whole city for such a stone.'

'Why?' asked Simone.

'Perhaps he had too much poison in his bones, or too much grief.'

'Rubies can cure such things?' asked Simone.

'Jewels have strange powers,' Jacopo argued. 'They say that coral tied to the neck drives away troublesome dreams and the nightly fears of children, and that creeping things fly from the scent of jet.'

'How reassuring.'

Paolo looked once more at the ruby, close against his eye. 'This is the true stone.'

'You are correct,' said Jacopo, momentarily impressed.

Simone beamed with pride. 'I told you he would be of benefit to you.'

Jacopo was still uncertain. 'But I am also told you cannot see into the distance. How will you tell me of dangers?'

'You will have to tell yourself,' Paolo replied.

The men were shocked by his directness.

'Then why should I not take a boy who can see perfectly well?'

'Because none other has Paolo's gifts,' said Simone.

'And he is of good temperament?'

'Exemplary . . .'

'For a Christian, which does not say very much.'

Simone smiled. 'There are good Christians.'

'Then I hope one day you will show one to me . . .'

Jacopo turned to Paolo. 'How do you know such things?'

'Because I see closely it is all I see.'

Jacopo watched the way Paolo still looked at the glass and the jewels. There was a ferocity of concentration in him that he had never seen before. 'We will make a strange pair of men. I cannot see close, and you cannot see into the distance . . .'

'Then you will take him?' asked Simone.

Jacopo shrugged. 'My life is risk; and I have never had a son. Let us journey together.' He seemed to have made the decision on a whim, and began to explain the terms of employment.

Paolo was to be a personal servant during the Sabbath and a companion during the week. He was asked to check that the prayer and festival books were always close by and would have to light fires, hold anything that needed to be carried, convey messages, and, most importantly, keep Jacopo's purse on the day of delight.

He told Paolo how they would stay in Jewish communities with his family, friends, and trading partners wherever they could: Jacopo de Nathan in Ragusa, Levi di Jacopo in Candia, Domenico Gualdi in Negroponte.

'You have done this journey before?' Paolo asked.

'Many times.'

'How long will it take?'

'It depends upon our fortune. Nine or ten months to reach the limit of our journey, if we are quick and the Lord wills it . . .'

'And the same to return?'

'Again, if we are blessed: *The earth of the Lord is full of the goodness of the Lord.*'

'And you trade in jade?'

'I do.'

Jacopo pulled out a piece to show him, and Paolo looked at its unusually veined luminosity, as pale as the flesh of a corpse.

'But this cannot become paint, of course,' Jacopo concluded, putting the jade back in its velvet pouch.

'No,' said Simone. 'As you know, I have asked Paolo to find a different shade: the blue of the heavens, the colour of eternity.'

'A modest proposal,' smiled Jacopo.

'I will know it when I see it,' said Paolo.

'Then I hope we agree when we find it.'

ಜಜ

Three weeks later Simone accompanied Paolo as far as Ancona where he would join the boat to take him to

Constantinople. Then he would continue overland across Persia to Cathay, completing their journey in Tun-huang where the trade routes met.

The harbour lay on the northeastern shore and was filled with boats that loomed above and sank below, studded with caulkers, carpenters, and cord-makers, metal-workers, shipwrights and blacksmiths all working as if a second flood were about to strike.

'This ship is insured for three hundred ducats. Imagine,' Simone explained, pointing at a large merchant galley. 'And this for two hundred. Venetian, of course.' He drew Paolo's attention to a twenty-eight-oar brigantine. 'Either boat could take you to the edge of the world with good enough men.'

He stopped alongside their trading galley, and waved to the captain as he supervised the loading of salt for ballast, sacks of grain, and bales of woollen cloth.

'Do you know him?' asked Paolo.

'Of course not. But he needs to know that we are important.'

They waited as a small group of sailors passed, singing a hymn to St Phocas for protection.

'Please.' Simone gestured, pointing to the walkway.

As Paolo climbed onto the ship, he could hardly believe that he had dared to embark on such a journey. What was he doing? He looked up and tried to make out its highest point, the *gabbia*, and the maintopmast topcastle. It looked higher even than the campanile on Murano. A great web of rope, hemp, hessian, and sail opened up above him. The lines blurred off into the distance, a strange infinity against the sky.

Simone now made the captain's acquaintance, arranging payments, checking the direction and duration of the journey.

'Stefano!' the captain called.

A boy, perhaps eleven years old, with a pockmarked face, raced up from the gangway.

'Show this boy the ship.'

'Yes, Captain.'

Stefano took Paolo to the windward side of the main-mast, asking him to look up to the topgallant to see the leonine flag of St Mark fluttering above. The bright blue of the sky was cut by a confusion of rigging: bowlines, ratlines, shrouds, lifts, and stays, and Stefano pointed out the main forecastle, beakhead, and rigging rail; the bowsprit, sprit yard, foremast, mizzen, and bonaventure. He showed Paolo how to look through the blindage, the removable archery screen through which bowmen would fire on any attackers, and told him how important it was to keep out of the way of men working rope and sail. He then took Paolo along a companion ladder down through a hatch into the darkness of the lower decks.

'I'll show you every beam, bitt, and bunker,' he laughed and recounted travellers' tales of what such adventure might mean: of earthquakes forty cubits high, of whales nine hundred feet long, and of eels which, he had heard, could choke a man even after they had been eaten, writhing and twisting their way inside the throat of their victims. People had returned from the east with stories of giants with teeth a hundred times the size of a man's; of cannibals and pigmies, sorcerers and soothsayers; of vast oceans, and mountains that touched the sky; of winds that could make a man fly, and of rains that could wash away whole towns.

On the rowing deck the oarsmen were already lining up on the benches. The air was damp with sweat, and there was little room to move or breathe. Paolo thought himself to be an intruder in a dark and secret world of men, violence, and adventure.

'Now,' said Simone, once they had returned to the upper deck, 'we must part. Take my purse.' He handed Paolo a leather wallet. 'It contains ten florins. Remember what I have taught you. Travel boldly and without fear. Find me the colour of eternity.'

'I cannot believe that I have agreed to this,' Paolo replied.

'Have courage. Who will have lived a life as interesting as yours? Think what a hero you will be on your return.'

'If I do return.'

'Of course you will.'

Simone did not quite know how to say goodbye and gave Paolo a playful punch on the shoulder which hurt far more than his pupil admitted. 'I will wave to you as the ship departs; perhaps you will not see it, but believe me, I will salute you.'

'Then I will look for your salutation.'

'Farewell.'

Simone leaned forward and attempted a paternal hug. Then there was a bell, a hauling at the anchor cable, and a sharp cry. All at once the men below began to row, chanting as they did so, pulling away with the tide, leaving all that was light. The figures on the shore were blurred and indistinct, and Paolo looked out into the path of the sea ahead. He felt the waters becoming thicker underneath as the ship struggled to make headway through treacherous channels. Out to the north lay a stretch of sandbanks, bleached gold by the evening sun, standing proud against the wash of the sea. He tried to look back to the city once more, in order to remember what they were leaving, holding it in his head, but it was already too late. He could not see Simone at all. Everything had become faint.

He made his way down onto the lower deck and asked Stefano if he should not try to find Jacopo.

'The old Jew? Let me take you to him.'

When he found his patron at last Paolo noticed that Jacopo had pushed back his sleeves and strapped one length of leather containing a prayer box to his left arm and another around his head. He stood with his feet together, hands folded over his heart, facing Jerusalem. As he spoke the words of the Amidah he bowed four times.

He prayed without acknowledging Paolo's presence.

'They that go down to the sea in ships, that do business in great waters – these saw the works of the Lord, and

*his wonders in the deep; for he commanded, and raised
the stormy wind, which lifted up the waves thereof.*

*'They mounted up to heaven, they went down to the
deeps; their souls melted away because of trouble; they
reeled to and fro, and staggered like a drunken man, and
all their wisdom was swallowed up – they cried unto the
Lord in their trouble, and he brought them out of their
distresses. He made the storm a calm, so that the waves
thereof were still. Then were they glad because they were
quiet, and he led them unto their desired haven. Let
them give thanks unto the Lord for his mercy, and for his
wonderful works to the children of men!'*

When he had finished, Jacopo turned to face Paolo.
'Sit down where you can and eat with me. I have challah.'
His voice softened. 'Marinated herring. Even some kich-
lach biscuits.'

'What are they?'

'Ah.' Jacopo smiled. 'I see that I have much to
teach you.'

He took off his prayer shawl, washed his hands from
a jug, dried them on a towel, and then sprinkled salt
over the bread.

'I cannot imagine the length of the journey,' said Paolo.

'You must have faith. *The fear of man brings a snare;
but whoever puts his trust in the Lord shall be safe.'*

'The Book of Proverbs.'

'You know the passage?' Jacopo was both curious and
amused. 'Of course; you believe in *that man.'*

'As my mother has told me.'

'The man who promised heaven within a generation.'

'I believe so.'

'But where is it? I cannot see it.'

'I have been taught that it is not for this earth.'

Jacopo smiled as if Paolo had fallen into his trap. 'But he told his followers – *Verily I say unto you, This generation shall not pass, till all these things be fulfilled*. How can he have been the Messiah, if we are still waiting for such deliverance? *And they shall see the Son of man coming in the clouds of heaven with power and great glory. And he shall send his angels with a great sound of a trumpet, and they shall gather together his elect from the four winds*.'

'You have read this?' asked Paolo.

'And I have found it wanting. His promise has already failed.'

'Then, as my mother believes, we must trust and love.'

Jacopo laughed. 'I do not want to insult your mother, but I do not see much trust and love from those of your faith. You preach poverty but covet wealth; you speak of forgiveness but your behaviour is otherwise. You say that we Jews are rapacious but you come to us for loans; you study with us but declare the Talmud to be blasphemous; and then, if that is not enough, we are persecuted . . .'

'I have not seen this . . .' said Paolo.

'If a Jew is bountiful then he is seeking to corrupt; if he is cautious then he is considered miserly. If he is proud then he is too proud; but if he is humble then he is too humble. Even if he is baptised into your faith he is still considered a Jew.'

'And yet Christ was a Jew.'

'He was,' said Jacopo. 'Perhaps you can remind the Christians we meet on our journey of that truth.'

∞

Just before nightfall Paolo climbed back up to the main deck and then onto the beakhead under the foremast. He watched the sky shade into dusk, filling both sea and horizon with the deepest and darkest of blues. He tried to understand what it was like to live without sight of landfall, alone in the vast expanse of ocean.

And, as he looked out into the night, he realised that his world had expanded far, far away from his own small life, wider than he had ever expected, out into an immensity.

CONSTANTINOPLE

The ship was swift under sail and made good progress towards Ragusa on the Dalmatian coast. Paolo soon learned to adjust to the crowded conditions, the stench of men and animals, and the meagre food; but the contrast between the darkness below decks and the brightness above hurt his eyes. He longed for a fixed sense of place where he could choose between light and shadow; for the freedom to travel in another direction; for solitude. He realised that the only way in which he could survive would be to be as discreet as possible and to make himself as familiar with the ship as if he were blind, memorising dimension and direction, learning the routine rhythms of work, sail, food, labour, and rest.

His first duty was to unload provisions as Jacopo sold wine and bought silver. He was to keep a record of every transaction and check their goods each day, inspecting cloth for damage and food for decay, re-stoppering bottles of oil and securing flagons of wine.

As they travelled Jacopo began to feel strangely responsible for his charge, worrying if he was wearing sufficient clothing or if he might become chilled. He was watchful of their diet, suggesting that Paolo eat not meat but fish cooked in wine according to his wife Sofia's recipe. He should also take as much fruit as possible in order to keep his kidneys healthy and his water clear. By the time they reached Candia, Jacopo had become almost paternal, telling his companion to avoid all temptation from the women of the town because a bite from a Cretan woman's teeth could be as fatal as the pox from her favours.

Paolo had not yet seen any women to be tempted by and, because of his eyesight, had difficulty in looking at them at all. If he wanted to see a girl properly he had to stand so close that the object of his intended affection would immediately wonder what he was doing, suspecting him either of lechery or theft. The only chance of an encounter lay in the crowded markets of the ports and islands where women stopped to gather provisions. There he would seek out moments of beauty – the fall of hair, a perfect mouth, or the curve of a breast. Yet such times came so fleetingly, and the women seemed so remote, that Paolo doubted that he would ever know the delights of flesh against flesh. Nevertheless, Jacopo insisted that he remain vigilant. A man should do everything possible to avoid temptation and desire.

When asked how the terrors of lust might be avoided, Jacopo advised that the best course of action would be to cease shaving immediately and grow a beard, since, in his experience, the most lustful men were always clean shaven.

'A beard,' he told Paolo, 'is a mark of wisdom and maturity.'

Paolo replied that his skin was so pale and his hair so fair that he wondered if anyone would ever notice if he had a beard or not, but Jacopo was adamant that he make the attempt.

It was slow progress.

Each day Paolo touched his face to check that the beard was growing. He scratched the stubble so often that it began to look like a nervous gesture. He would peer down his nose to see the burgeoning hairs on his upper lip. The spikes were sharp blond, pale brown, even auburn. It was as if the beard were not his own and that a separate creature had taken possession of his face.

'I do not like it,' he told Jacopo, but his guardian insisted he continue, arguing that a beard not only conveyed wisdom and learning, but also gave character to a man's profile. It compensated for any loss of hair on the scalp, for the chin and the cheeks possessed far more vigorous follicles. It was also economical, saving money in the acquiring of knives and time spent shaving; and, most importantly, it would not only protect the face from the heat of the desert, but also avoid giving offence in the land of Mohammed.

Jacopo was quite obsessed with the subject. Male lizards, he told Paolo, grew beards in courtship displays;

Noah and Methuselah must both have had beards that were over nine hundred years old; and the female Christian saints, Paula and Uncumber, had both escaped being ravished by spontaneously growing miraculous moustaches.

By the time they reached Constantinople, Paolo's beard was in positive sprout and he had almost begun to enjoy the adventure. He had never seen such a majestic array of buildings: the city laid out in splendour across the waterfront, its mosques and minarets glistening in the evening light as if created by a single wave of God's hand.

Once they had disembarked the two men found themselves in a maze of narrow streets filled with strolling musicians, itinerant jugglers, sudden crowds, and intense heat. There were pickle sellers, spice merchants, halvamakers, and children hawking cherries and pistachios. There were barbers, bakers, butchers, and babies; prophets and priests, hajjis and hojas, judges and jewellers. Gem cutters and glyptographers worked turquoise from Anatolia, amber from the Baltic, agate and amethyst from beyond the seas. Jacopo stopped at each stall, measuring each of the stones, weighing and judging, pressing them to the side of his cheek to feel their temperature, continually assessing the validity of each sample on offer.

Constantinople, he told Paolo, was a place of glory and of crime, where the best and the worst in human nature combined: the holiest men meditated amongst criminals; the most saintly women were forced to walk past murderers and whores. Paolo looked at the women who stood in the streets with their breasts exposed and wondered how much it might cost to touch them. It was hard for him to discern either their age or beauty, and every time they came close, Jacopo ushered them quickly away in disgust.

He warned Paolo that this was a city of heat, noise, and strangeness, so loud, so crowded, and so confused that none could trust their sight or hearing, such was the nature of its blast and din. If the trumpet announcing the Day of Judgment were sounded he swore that it would pass unnoticed.

Nothing was permanent, as if the city could never be stilled. Each person travelled for fear they might miss the end of the world, the solution to misery, or the key to happiness. They were looking for miracles, journeying in desperation to find somewhere, anywhere, other than where they were. Stalls and benches were laid out to soothe fears and answer any question a man or woman might choose to ask: 'How long will I live?' 'Will I stay healthy?' 'How will I die?' Others were more specific. 'Shall I buy a farm?' 'Should I marry my cousin?' 'Am I the father of my wife's child?' There were fortune-tellers, palm-readers, and soothsayers all seeing into the future by different means: by contemplation, trance, or divine inspiration; by holding a piece of clothing or jewellery; by feeling muscles, drawing lots, turning cards; or by the simple observation of a flight of doves.

Hour after hour people gave up their secrets and then listened as their personalities were revealed and confirmed: their weaknesses, hopes, and fears; their loves and losses, dreams and disasters. Charlatan after charlatan confirmed that although their clients could be outwardly confident they could be as vulnerable as children; that women were dissatisfied with their hair and men feared losing theirs; that some had been afraid of dogs as children, some needed to live near water, and others had a scar on their left knee. Christians were told that a woman called Maria had been, or would one day be, important to them. Jews were informed that a distant relative, David probably, was often in their thoughts. And it was confirmed to Mahometans that the Prophet was ever watchful.

As they ate sweets of halva and fried dough, marzipan and sugar, Paolo asked if he too could find out about his future, and even his past. Would he ever meet his true mother or father? Would he find the blue stone? Would he ever know love?

'It is not good to know of the future,' Jacopo answered. 'It is for God alone.'

'But what of the past? What if I do not understand that?'

'You have a lifetime to discover your own past,' Jacopo replied.

'But I want to know now.'

Jacopo looked worried. 'You know these men are charlatans.'

'Then why do people go?'

'Like you, they need hope.'

'Then give me hope.'

At last Jacopo relented, telling Paolo that he would pay for a consultation with a Latin-speaking soothsayer if only to teach his charge how fraudulent the world could be. He gave Paolo three ducats and they approached a tent that seemed to glow like gold.

'Consult your destiny,' he advised.

Inside, just behind a table, sat a man with a narrow face and a beard that was almost blue. He was dressed in a bright-yellow hooded cape. His eyes were closed, and he appeared to be in a trance. The man lowered his head towards a small crucible in front of him, and inhaled a substance that looked remarkably like black pepper. He then sat back, stretching his arms out wide, and emitted the longest and loudest sneeze Paolo had ever heard.

'*Veni*,' said the man.

He brought out two further crucibles and explained, in Latin, that he could tell much of a man's future simply by measuring the direction and duration of the human sneeze. It would cost Paolo five ducats. This might seem expensive, but he would be able to tell in which direction his guest must travel in order to fulfil his destiny, and for how long. He could even, in certain circumstances, predict the duration of the journey and when a man might be expected to return home.

'I only have three ducats.'

'Very well. Give me what you can.'

Paolo paid the money and stood before the crucibles. The man in the yellow gown brought forth what looked like a compass, and encouraged Paolo to begin.

The first crucible was thick with the scent of paprika. Paolo inhaled, and then turned to his right, sneezing away from the table three times.

'South,' shouted the man.

He brought the second crucible to Paolo and invited him to sniff once more. This was pepper.

Paolo inhaled, and his whole body convulsed. His eyes began to stream with the heat and the powder. He felt an enormous sneeze welling inside him until it could be contained no more.

The resulting sensile explosion was so strong that it lifted him in the air, twisting his body round upon itself.

Paolo sneezed five times.

'East,' instructed the man. 'Five months.'

'No more,' cried his patient.

'One more,' instructed the sorcerer. 'It is your destiny.'

Paolo looked at the bowl of yellow powder before him. Could it be cumin? He inhaled as lightly as he could, and then began to sneeze again; his body shuddered, and he found himself back in the position in which he had first entered the room.

The man held out a hot towel. 'Blow,' he ordered. 'Clear yourself.'

Paolo obeyed. His eyes burned with pain and heat.

'Now rest,' ordered the sorcerer. 'Sit in this chair, and

close your eyes.' Paolo felt his eyes cool, as the man laid what appeared to be cucumber across them.

'It will be a long journey,' the sorcerer began; 'and it will have dangers. Much heat. You will be very hot. Perhaps at one point you will think that you are dying.'

'You can tell all this from the way in which I sneeze?'

'No. That is destiny. But I advise you to travel south at first, with whatever friends you have. Do not be alone. Then you must, and you will, travel east. Far, far east. For many months.'

'Five months . . .' Paulo ventured.

'Probably. The sneezes seldom lie . . .'

'And then?'

'You finished sneezing in the same position. This means that you will return home. And you will see more clearly . . .'

'You know my sight is poor?'

'On the contrary. I know your sight is sharp. Sharper than a hawk's.'

'But only close.'

'Then that is how you must look.'

'And will I find the colour that I seek?'

'That I cannot tell.'

'Shall I know my true mother or father? Shall I find love? Will I return safely?'

'You will find what you need; and learn to live with what you have.'

'Is that it?' asked Paolo, disappointed by such a conclusion.

'Think on these things,' said the man. 'Great things have been revealed.'

ოი

Jacopo took advantage of Paolo's disappointment by telling him that the folly of such charlatans should only make him concentrate harder on true religion. These men plundered human superstition and distracted their gullible patients from the rewards of faith.

But as they walked through the city amidst the ruins of fallen empires and extinct beliefs, Paolo began to think increasingly that religion too had its absurdities. He had visited the Christian relics held in the city: the twelve baskets from the feeding of the five thousand, the head of John the Baptist, fragments of the True Cross, and even a phial of milk expressed from the breast of the Virgin Mary. This puzzled him, for he had already been shown an altogether different head of John the Baptist on his travels, as well as the foot of St Stephen and six breasts belonging to St Agatha, which would surely make her reincarnation problematic.

Paolo wondered why people prayed to these saints. If they were already in heaven, interceding for those left on earth, then how had they been resurrected? Were their fingernails, shoulder blades, jawbones, and breasts still left on earth? Was heaven filled with saints who were incomplete?

He thought of Simone and his attempt to paint heaven; how could such an idea ever be depicted? The colour he had been sent to find would have to be a shade of infinite breadth and depth in which there could be no tone or shade but one equal, everlasting sense of rest. Surely it was impossible.

On the eve of the Sabbath, Paolo accompanied Jacopo along the city walls towards a synagogue in Balat. As they walked, his patron insisted that Paolo worried too much about the literal truth of faith and should not expect the divine to be understood by human reason.

'We must hope and pray. *Give unto the Lord the glory due unto his name: bring an offering, and come into his courts.*'

'But what if we are wrong?' Paolo asked. 'I cannot imagine heaven at all.'

'And what if we are right?' Jacopo replied. 'Imagine all the pleasure, all the peace, and all the joy that there has ever been on earth: the purest moments of bliss experienced by those who have already lived and those who will live. Gather up this indescribable beauty, the sum total of all the truth and glory that will ever be known, and consider it but a shadow of the divine ecstasy to come. To doubt is vanity. God asks for faith, virtue, and the humility of patience. Surely that is not so difficult, given the heavenly reward that lies in store?'

He turned and made his way into the synagogue. 'Do not be afraid of faith.'

Paolo sat on a low stone wall. 'If only it was easier,' he thought. 'If only I could know it to be true.'

৵৹৻

As he waited outside, Paolo could just make out a blurred group of men entering a large complex of buildings on the other side of the square. When one of them stopped to adjust the straps on his sandals, and Paolo asked where he was going, the stranger made himself understood by gesture, indicating that this was a *hamam*, and that if he wanted a Turkish bath then he should join the other men at once. The potential bather seemed so welcoming, and the heat and dust of the day had taken such a toll that Paolo could not help but accept the invitation.

In the outer courtyard men were taking off their clothes and signalled that Paolo should do likewise. Even though he could not see well, he was amazed by the relaxed way in which his fellow bathers displayed themselves, readjusting their testicles, flicking each other playfully with towels. Paolo took off his leggings and sandals, his shirt and trousers, and was given a loose cloth to tie around his waist before being shown by an attendant into the hall of the bath.

Here he was washed down with a sponge, and showered with warm water before being directed into a room steaming with hot coals. The attendant indicated that he should spend ten minutes in the room and then leave.

Paolo felt the steam rise slowly around him, and globules of sweat drop from his body. His eyelids began to ache and he could no longer see the other men in the room. When he judged that ten minutes had passed, he clasped his towel to his waist and made for the door.

Uncertain which way to turn, he found himself in front of a series of doorways. He passed through the central arch and entered a small room with a low table.

Through the heat and the steam he noticed a small woman with a high voice suggesting that he should lie down on a white cloth before her.

Paolo lay down on his stomach, but the attendant turned him onto his back and began to work up a lather with her hands in a bucket of soap and water. Then she started to massage his right foot, working her way up through the shin and calf to the knee and then on to the thigh. Paolo felt the warmth and the sensuality of the deep massage and then, to his horror, as the attendant progressed to his upper thigh, he felt himself begin to stiffen. There was nothing he could do to stop it. He was having an erection.

The attendant moved on to his left leg, soaping the underside, the thigh, and even his testicles. She had already pulled at each toe, elongating each joint, and now Paolo began to fear for his manhood. The intense and necessary excitement in his groin was overwhelming.

'You want me finish?' she asked quietly in Latin.

Paolo thought she had only just started.

'No,' said Paolo, and immediately she began to work on his arms and his chest.

Was that what he had meant? He liked her touching him down there.

'Yes,' said Paolo suddenly. 'Yes, yes, yes.'

'You want me finish?' the attendant asked again.

'Yes,' said Paolo, understanding at last, and the attendant returned once more to his groin, stroking, rubbing and pulling until finally Paolo could no longer contain his pleasure, and made his own unique contribution to the soapy lather around him.

'Good,' said the attendant, who now crouched down behind him, took his head in her hands, and rubbed a wet paste of henna into his hair, moustache, and beard. Paolo closed his eyes.

The attendant then turned him onto his front and began work once more on his legs, pulling at each toe, pummelling his calves, and pinching at his buttocks.

'Rest,' the woman instructed in a piping voice.

Paolo tried to loosen his arms but he could not help thinking about what had happened. He did not know whether to feel embarrassment or pleasure.

The attendant now began to pumice his body, cleansing the dead flesh, washing away the dust of travel. Paolo did not think he had ever been so clean in his life. She then made him sit up, wrapped in a towel, and led him to a large pool of water.

'In,' she ordered, and Paolo found himself slipping into a cistern of water so cold it made him cower. He felt himself shrink before her.

'Out,' she commanded, covering him in yet another towel.

'Now lie down and rest.'

As he lay down the woman placed further towels upon him so that he felt he had been wrapped in his winding sheet. Perhaps he was already dead, and this experience had been but a dream.

After ten minutes, the attendant returned.

'Finish,' she said, holding his clothes, ready for Paolo to dress once more.

Paolo opened his eyes and rubbed them. Wearily he reached for his clothes. He put on his shirt and trousers and could see that the attendant was still waiting.

'Happy?' she asked.

'Yes,' Paolo replied, but then he noticed that something was not quite right. He leaned forward. His short-haired, bright-eyed attendant with the high voice and the fine features had no breasts.

Paolo took a deep breath, rose, and left the *hamam*. His first sexual experience had been with a eunuch.

PERSIA

When it was time to leave Constantinople, Paolo and Jacopo took a boat up the Bosphorus and sailed along the Black Sea to Trabzon. Then they journeyed south-east towards Tabriz, following the path of the silk route.

They travelled on horseback through valleys of apples, apricots, and pomegranates, and over the barren mountains of eastern Anatolia. By day they saw few people other than shepherds herding flocks or children gathering wild flowers, sucking the juice from their stalks; but by night they would sleep in the *Han* and *Rabat* of the caravanserai, among courtyards filled with noise, heat, and activity. On one side lay dormitories, baths, and bedrooms; on the other stood workshops, stores, and kitchens. A vast gateway at the back led to stables where blacksmiths hammered out new horseshoes, and farriers tended to the animals. In the middle of each courtyard stood a richly decorated *mescat*, a pavilion-mosque that appeared to float on supporting stone arches. The call of the muezzin mingled with distant music, dancing, fights, and laughter as the cooks roasted lamb for their guests, and traders jostled to exchange silver from the mines of Argyropolis or turquoise from Kerman.

Paolo soon learned to adjust to the differing diets of each new community, eating dried beef spiced with fenugreek, sheep's brain salad, or honey made from Pontic azalea which, it was said, could turn a man mad. The heat made him continually thirsty, and the more he travelled the more he realised how simple a man's needs could become: food and shelter, sleep and water.

They stopped for two days of rest at Mount Ararat, and, as Jacopo prayed, Paolo watched a group of women weaving carpets under a magnolia tree, working each strand dyed with indigo, madder, or camomile through a web of taut strings on their looms. At the centre of every design stood the tree of life. The women were creating heaven with their hands, paradise under their feet.

As he tried to focus on their work Paolo wondered if he had almost forgotten the purpose of his journey. He was lost between arrival and departure, beginning and end, as if his travels might never cease. One of the weaving women appeared to think he was dreaming. When she looked up and asked where he was going he couldn't quite remember.

'I am looking for the colour of heaven.'

She nodded, but Paolo was not sure if she had understood him.

'You will find it soon enough.' The woman spoke a little Latin.

'It is close?'

'Closer than you think. We all make the same journey. From God to God.'

Paolo started to move away, but the woman gestured that he should sit with her. She patted the bench and made room, and he settled down beside her to watch the weaving. As he did so, he realised that he had never been so close to a woman other than his mother and he felt strangely calm. Children played around them, and one brought him a drink of pomegranate juice.

'My daughter,' the woman explained. Then she pointed at the boys. 'My sons.'

Paolo was suddenly fearful that the man of the house might return and see him sitting with his wife. He should get up and return to Jacopo, he knew, but he found that he did not want to do so. He was content.

The woman gestured that he should drink, and Paolo brought the dark-red liquid to his lips. It was unexpectedly cool, thick, rich, and sweet.

'Each pomegranate should be eaten one seed at a time,' the woman was saying, 'one ruby after another, for it was from such a seed that paradise grew.'

Paolo nodded. The woman returned to her work and Paolo felt even more at ease with her as she wove, her slender fingers handling the thread with confident speed.

He could feel her thigh next to his and her headscarf brushed against his shoulder. Her dark-green eyes had a softness that told him everything would surely be well. He could stay. He no longer needed to worry about the cares of the world.

Paolo knew that this was a moment in time, and that it must surely pass, but he sensed that he had been given a glimpse of contentment. If only he could know it for longer.

He finished his pomegranate juice, thanked the woman, and placed his cup down on the bench. He made a short bow and the woman held out her hand. Paolo reached forward, and because his head was still low, he let the back of her hand brush against his lips.

His first kiss.

He looked up to meet the woman's eyes, and she smiled, withdrew her hand, and gave him a little wave. Paolo was almost emboldened to kiss her on the lips but the children ran around her, singing and dancing, and he could hear a baby crying in the clay dwelling behind. It was time to leave.

Later, as he prepared the food that night, roasting skewers of chicken, aubergine, and green pepper over the fire, and Jacopo was telling him how much he missed the company of his wife Sofia, Paolo began to wonder if he would ever find love. Because they never stayed in any place for more than one or two nights it was impossible to meet people for any length of time. Both men had suspended their lives for the duration of the journey, as if they had embarked on a parallel existence which bore no relation to the world they had come from. They were adrift from their own history.

೧೦೩

By the time they reached Tabriz Jacopo told Paolo that they would have to change their horses for camels and employ a guide to take them across the great wastes of the desert. They could no longer travel alone.

'One must take great care,' his patron warned. 'You cannot know a man until you have been in the desert with him.'

They made their way in the heat of the afternoon to the great mosque and citadel in the centre of the city. Paolo had never seen such an expansive building, with its towering minarets, its marble-paved courtyard, and its alabaster-columned arcade. The ablution pool was so large that a barge could sail across it. Outside, a group of men were sitting at some tables in the shade, cracking pistachio nuts and drinking yoghurt. Some sprang up immediately they saw the two foreigners, eager to state both their knowledge of the desert and their linguistic ability; others seemed unconcerned whether they were employed or not, as if the whole concept was beneath them.

Jacopo approached one of the oldest and smallest people Paolo thought he had ever seen. A Seljuk Turk, the man must have been at least sixty years of age, with a well-lined face that had been wizened by the sun. He wore a dark-brown *kameez* shirt, baggy *shalwar* trousers, and a voluminous black turban. Every item of his clothing appeared to be two or three sizes too big for him. He had an almost careless air, as if nothing need ever be hurried, and he sat apart from the others, smoking a pipe under an almond tree.

Although his beard was trim, his eyes were yellow and bloodshot, which made Paolo think that he would make the most unlikely of guides.

'Salek?' enquired Jacopo, speaking in basic Persian. 'I thought you were dead.'

The man took the pipe from his mouth and squinted up. 'I am alive, *inshallah* . . .'

'You remember me?'

'Of course. I forget nothing.'

'I may need your help once more.'

The man returned to his pipe, untroubled by such a request. 'I do not know where you wish to go. And I am old.'

'But you are still a guide?'

'If I am anything; yes, that is true.'

Paolo wondered why Jacopo was keen to employ a man so reluctant to travel.

'Let us eat together and talk. My journey will bring both adventure and profit.'

'I have learned not to trust people who offer adventure, and I am too old for profit.'

'Then perhaps it will not cost so much,' answered Jacopo with alacrity.

'I see you have forgotten. Because I care less, it will cost more.'

'No,' replied Jacopo. 'That is one thing I have not forgotten.'

'I always cost too much. That is why you trust me.' For the first time Salek smiled. Then he noticed Paolo.

'Who is the boy?'

'My companion.'

'Then why do you need me?'

'Paolo is travelling in search of colour, the blue of Badakhshan. Then we must continue to Cathay, for jade.'

'A long journey.'

'I know it will be expensive,' said Jacopo.

'But why should you worry?' asked Salek. 'You are rich.'

'Not as rich as you think,' answered Jacopo.

'But richer than you admit.' Salek smiled. 'Come, let us eat.'

They walked away to discuss their terms of business over a meal of bread, olives, yoghurt, and stuffed vine leaves. Salek demanded authority for the route chosen and a special price for each day, whereas Jacopo wanted to offer him a total for the journey and the freedom to stop for longer where trade was good. As they haggled both men knew that they would eventually agree, and that the debate was little more than a reminder of their respective positions. Salek spoke Latin, Persian, and the language of Cathay, and it was clear that their journey would be impossible without him. Jacopo had simply to secure the best price and agree on the number of miles they would cover each day.

Then there was the question of the animals. The next morning Salek took both Paolo and Jacopo to the market where a group of disdainful camels lowed, bellowed, and kicked out at all who came near them.

The men kept a safe distance and walked round each animal in turn, as if measuring their ability to be subdued. Jacopo stood apart and asked if each one could be made to kneel. He told Paolo to stand as close as he could and examine the backs and withers, looking for any nicks, cuts, or wounds which might worsen or become infected in the desert. Then, when the animal stood again, they looked at the legs, to ensure that they were not crooked, excessively fat, or might hobble. Salek scrutinised the inside of the front legs for signs of rubbing, looked into each camel's eyes to see that they were bright and alert, and patted each hump to check that it was firm. Then he made them walk, trot, and canter, slow, stop, sit, and rise again, ensuring that the journey would not be endangered by the weakness of any one.

Once they had been purchased (and Salek had received his commission), the camels were led to the courtyard where the expedition was to begin. Their knees were tied before nightfall to prevent them escaping. As soon as it was light, they were fed and watered before being loaded with all their possessions. It was the first time that Paolo had seen the need of an animal put before the wants of men.

'They are our means of survival,' Salek insisted. 'We are nothing without them.'

Then he checked the equipment: portable tents, sleeping sheets, and poles; ropes for climbing, picks, and axes; flagons of water, barley, grain, and oil; plates, bowls, ladles, and pans. Each man's kit bag was to contain two water bottles, a knife, a swathe of cloth against heat and cold, candles, flints, undergarments, and gloves. Paolo looked into his knapsack and checked he still had the coloured glass for trade and the leather purse Simone had given him. Salek brought him clothes for the heat and the journey, a long-sleeved *kameez* shirt which stretched down to his thighs, and loose *shalwar* trousers to keep his legs cool.

At last they were ready to depart, but when Paolo tried to climb onto the back of his camel, the animal seemed decidedly unfriendly.

'Mount from the left,' Salek instructed.

The camel ducked and moved his head away, shirking Paolo's efforts, determined that he should not be ridden. 'Take its upper lip,' Salek urged, as the camel roared and lunged.

Paolo had never seen such a mouth.

'Pull it back. Pull the head round,' ordered Salek.

The camel squirmed.

'Put your left foot on his foreleg. Hard.'

Paolo tentatively placed his foot on the camel's reclined left foreleg.

'Now swing your right leg over the pommel of the saddle.' Salek mimed the action.

Paolo hesitated.

'I will show you.' Salek mounted his camel in three swift movements: hand on mouth, leg on foreleg, swing onto saddle. Then came the command to move forward.

'Now, Paolo,' Salek said. 'Do as I have done.'

Paolo jumped up onto his camel. Its rear legs lurched up suddenly, first throwing him forward and then violently back.

'Move with the animal,' said Jacopo gravely. 'Feel the rhythm.'

'There is no rhythm!' shouted Paolo. 'It's lurching.'

'Let him know you,' advised Salek. 'Be calm. Everyone is nervous at first. But in three days you will be able to place your fingers in his nostrils, look him in the eye, and establish your authority.'

'Walk on, walk on,' Paolo commanded, nervously.

The animal turned, bit him in the leg, and began to advance.

Clearly the nostrils would have to wait.

ೞ

On leaving Tabriz, Salek told Paolo they would travel southeast through Persia towards Rhages and then make their way across the north of the desert to Masshad. He rode at the head of the caravan. Behind him followed six camels laden with merchandise. Jacopo brought up the rear. Order was kept by a fine woollen string which flowed back along the line, threaded through each camel's nose, and along each saddle, tied off on a large bell attached to the neck of the last animal. This produced a low even sound as they travelled, letting Salek know that all was in order. It gave rhythm to their progress as they walked up hills and trotted on the flat. Any change in the ringing of the bell necessitated an inspection, and Salek was adamant that their party keep as close together as possible.

They ate a mixture of ground barley and warm water, with dates when they could find them, and drank sweet tea. Salek taught Paolo how to eat slowly, letting both the food and the drink take effect between each mouthful so that the body had time to replenish itself. He must feel neither empty nor replete. A breaker of water should be sipped. Bread should be savoured. Their provisions were as important as their jewels.

Salek stopped only to check the animals, to smoke a pipe, and to pray. Jacopo made his devotions three times a day, insisting on the evening *Ma'ariv*, the morning *Shacharit*, and the afternoon *Mincha*; whereas Salek required five sets of prayers thanking Allah for survival each evening and asking for his blessing throughout each day.

'The soul must be guarded,' he told Paolo, 'like a house from the rain.'

Because Salek prayed more often than Jacopo, Paolo noticed that the Jew would then fight back by deliberately praying for longer.

'My help is from the Lord who made heaven and earth.
Cast thy burden upon the Lord, and he shall sustain thee.

Mark the innocent man and behold the upright; for the latter end of that man is peace. Trust in the Lord, and do good; dwell in the land and feed upon faithfulness.'

But Salek would not be outdone.

'O Allah, I ask for your pardon and wellbeing in this life and in the hereafter.

'O Allah, cover my faults and soothe my fears.

'O Allah, protect me from before me and from behind me, and from my right and from my left, and from above me and from beneath me. I seek my refuge in you.'

As they travelled further, the journey seemed infinite; as if Paolo, Salek, and Jacopo had lost themselves in a dream without end. There were no landmarks to guide them, and each horizon only introduced another. At times it appeared there were no colours except those between pale gold and burnt sienna. The camels stalked forward, padding silently in ranks of ochre, fawn, sand, and caramel, bleached by the noon sun, darkened by night.

In the valleys they felt sharp stones underfoot, mixed with decaying camel bones and animal skulls, revealed by fresh winds that whipped across the sands only to cover them over once more. The only trees had denuded barks, and leaned to the south, permanently bent by the force of the wind. Paolo thought they looked like a row of old men waiting to die.

Before they made camp, Salek would check for the

direction of any breeze, arranging goods, panniers, and equipment, always seeing to the animals first. The camels would feel for the softest ground, dropping onto their forelegs, and folding in their hind legs before craning out their necks and lowering their jaws. At last their eyes would close, as if this was not only the end of the day but the silence of their secrets. Their inscrutability would never be understood, for they were the only creatures to know the hundredth name of Allah.

Each night Paolo and Salek hobbled the animals, tying their knees with knotted ropes to prevent them escaping. Jacopo made small fires with twigs and camel dung and prepared what food they had, throwing rocks up into the palm trees to dislodge the dates. After they had eaten they washed their pans in the freezing sand, scraping off and burying the debris, and then lay down, as close as they could to the fires they had made, and tried to sleep, limbs exhausted, their knees and hips aching.

Seven days after they had left Rhages, the camels escaped.

Paolo woke early and immediately sensed that something was wrong. He circled the tent, hoping that he dreamed, wondering desperately how he could make time unravel and re-tie the animals, securing them ever more firmly.

But they were gone, and the sand had covered all sign of their tracks.

Paolo began to panic. He was lost in the middle of the desert, with little water and no animals. How long could they last? Two days, three? Would any other traveller find them? Salek had told him that the vastness of the desert made it easier to believe in God and the majesty of his creation; but now he felt only the terror of its emptiness. There was nothing in sight: no tree, no settlement, no people, no water, no animals, and no food.

He must set out and find the camels before the others woke, but which direction should he take? The heat haze of the early morning only made his sight even more blurred. As he stood thinking, uncertain which way to turn, his companions emerged from the tent.

'Where are the animals?' Salek cried. 'What have you done?'

'They have gone.'

'Where? Did you see them?'

'I awoke too late.'

Jacopo knew that he could not quarrel with the guide on whom his life depended, and so he turned his anger on Paolo. 'Can you not tell where they have gone?' His eyes squinted against the light. 'But then I forget, you can't see anything. Never trust a camel or a boy.'

'It is not my fault,' said Paolo. 'I tied them well, as I have been taught. I looked hard at each knot.'

Jacopo began to search through the camel bags and provisions on the ground. 'You don't see anything as other men do.'

'That's not true.'

'The truth is that we are lost and may die.'

'We are not lost. I will find them,' said Salek calmly. 'You stay. I will walk. Let me take the boy.'

Paolo gathered cloth for shade and picked up two skins filled with water. Salek waited and then beckoned for him to follow. 'We must find them before the sun is high; there is nowhere to rest from the heat.'

'I will wait and pray,' said Jacopo. 'Perhaps I should make ready and atone.'

'They have been gone only a few hours,' said Salek. 'There is no need to despair.'

They looked out at the vanishing infinity of sand.

'How can we know where to start?' asked Paolo.

'The animals may have sensed water,' Salek replied, 'and so we should travel south, over those dunes.'

Paolo could not believe that his guide was sure.

'This is our test,' said Salek. 'The desert forces us to find our courage and our faith. We must conserve our energy, keep water, and find shade where we can. Look for tracks or camel dung as we walk.'

The heat moved across the sands like a wave. If only it were the sea, Paolo thought, if only this sun could be its exact opposite, washing away the desperate dryness of the desert with the cool clarity of water.

They tried to keep a steady pace as they walked, fearful of slowing, and were accompanied by nothing but their own breath in the heat, their feet on the sand. They missed the slow rhythmic steps of the camels, and the reassuring sound of the bell.

It was a journey of heat and emptiness. Whenever

Paolo looked towards the horizon and saw smudges of darkness in the distance, nestling between sand and sky, and cried out to Salek, the answer would always be the same: 'Rocks, just rocks.'

Paolo tried not to despair, but as the day developed he began to drift, falling asleep in the heat, the light too bright for his eyes.

'Shade them,' said Salek. 'Use more cloth. The desert is both sun and death. We cannot look at either directly.'

Paolo realised that this was why Salek's clothes seemed always too large. He used the extra material for protection. 'How can you ever tell where we are?'

'It is my home.'

'All this?'

'Everything.'

It was as if they were the last men left on earth.

'Why are you so calm?' asked Paolo.

'Because I know we will not come to harm. Allah protects us. Even if we die, then the worst becomes the best. We will know paradise.'

The mention of death made Paolo aware, for the first time in his life, that he might die far sooner than he had ever imagined, here in this heat, his task unfulfilled. His legs were heavy, his back ached, and his mouth was dry. He began to think that the only way he could stay alive would be to think of something else, to distract his mind. He would have to force Salek to speak, for this silence was impossible. Even though it would hurt their throats they must surely talk, telling stories to save their lives.

'Speak to me of your home,' Paolo asked. 'Do you dream about it?' He wanted to ask, 'Where do you rest at the end of your travels?' but recognised he would have to conserve energy, using as few words as possible.

'I do not.'

'You have no house?' Paolo asked. 'No family, no wife, no love?'

Salek continued walking. 'I live the life of a traveller. And I had no choice.'

'Why?'

'Let us not discuss this.' He spoke as if the conversation were over, but then, after walking a few more paces in the heat, too tired to conceal the truth, he suddenly confessed. 'I lived in a village to the south, near the turquoise hills of Kerman. I killed a man. I had to leave.'

'Why?'

'He killed my father. I killed him. Then I left.'

This is not what I had imagined, thought Paolo. I am alone in the heat of the desert with a murderer. 'Will you return?' he asked.

'One day, perhaps, when all the others are dead.'

Paolo wanted to ask about family, love, and children, but as he was about to speak, Salek forestalled him. 'Please, no more questions. Silence is better.'

It was midday. The sun bleached the sand so vividly that Paolo imagined it was snow. He tried to concentrate on cold flat plains, white peaked mountains, and streams of water: anything to avoid the pain of such heat. 'Why are we doing this?' he asked. 'Why can we not admit that we are less than the desert?'

'Now you are learning humility,' Salek replied. 'Let us walk and be patient. If we cannot find the camels then we will die. But who is to say what is beyond each dune?'

'I never want to see sand again in my life.'

'Do not say such a thing. You will remember it always. A man who has seen such sights will never forget them. What kind of life would you have if you had seen none of this?'

'A comfortable life.'

'And a life not worth living,' Salek answered, nearing the peak of the dune. He smiled and waited for Paolo to join him.

'There.'

In the distance, Paolo could just make out the shapes of the animals under a solitary palm.

'They have found water.'

As Salek approached, one of the camels turned to look at him with an expression of careless bemusement, as if wondering why they had taken so long to catch up and enjoy the well.

Looking at the animals, Paolo was uncertain which of his emotions was the stronger: relief at their discovery, or anger that they appeared so contemptuous.

ಬಬ

Because the camels now began to moult, their backs chafing in the heat, Salek insisted that they reverse their routine, travelling by night and resting each morning. Paolo found sleep in the bright heat of the day almost impossible. He wrapped every part of his body against the sun, protecting himself from its rays with dark swathes of cotton, but still the light hurt his eyes. He could feel the temperature rise inexorably and then, just when he thought he could bear it no longer, evening would fall and it became cold so fast that he was suddenly freezing.

They were caught between extremes and at times Paolo was unable to tell the difference between the fire of the day and the ice of the night. Much of the water they found was brackish, the opium balm to ward off mosquitoes proved ineffective, and their supplies of food ran low. Now there was only enough water to moisten their lips. Each drop had to be conserved, every spring searched, and they dreamed of the dates they had shared in more fertile climes. The only signs of life were the bones of the camels who had gone before.

By now Salek had begun to teach Paolo the rudiments of Arabic. First, the names of food and provisions: bread, water, wheat, fruit, and wine. Then his articles of trade: glass, jewels, beads, and mirrors; silk, cotton, wool, and hemp. He learned how to count in several languages and how to trade: less, more, and how much? What were the hundred words he needed to know? The thousand? The five thousand? He tried to number and name the stars even though he could hardly tell them apart, and he was told of the importance of religious invocation in keeping the path of righteousness. *Praise to God. Thanks to God. God willing.*

Paolo wondered how many languages a man might need to travel across the world. His guide answered that a man might need a thousand, or he might need none – either in trade or in love. It did not matter.

When Paolo asked what that meant, Salek told him to wait until they reached Masshad. There he would show wonders, heaven on earth.

And so they headed further east, leaving the desert and passing through a series of rice fields and wooded hills where they saw wild boar and marmoset. Hunters offered them a share of their food, and they ate salads of fresh parsley, tarragon, chives, wild garlic, and mint. Yoghurt with beetroot or spinach was freely available in the small towns and villages along the route, and in the evenings they would indulge in great stews of *fesenjan*, poultry with ground walnut and pomegranate syrup sauce. On one road they passed a series of pigeon towers, built from brick and overlaid with plaster and lime. Salek explained that thousands of pigeons would nest in these towers, not for breeding or eating, but to provide guano with which to fertilise the local melon fields. Paolo vowed that he would never look at a melon in the same way again.

Eventually they could see the gilded dome and minarets of Masshad, the holiest city in Persia, with the great mosque and mausoleum of Reza at its centre, surrounded by gardens of jasmine, iris, lily, and rose. The main square was filled with pilgrims and with merchants selling rosaries, clay tablets, perfume, and green fabric swatches for touching the grilles of the holy sanctuaries. Others stood behind high piles of saffron or precious stone, herbs or jewels, and Jacopo inspected the samples of turquoise laid out on tables before them.

The three men slept in a *Rabat* outside the city, next to a rose garden. An avenue of white poplars led to a turquoise gate with Kufic inscriptions from the Qur'an, and then opened out into a small courtyard with a pool of water at its centre. The stream flowed into four channels, becoming the rivers of paradise: the Pison and the Gihon, the Hiddekel and the Euphrates.

It was perfectly proportioned, each measurement calculated upon the human body: an arm's length, a handspan, the height of both men and women. Each path was tiled with mosaic floors in geometric floral designs, matching, in stone, the lotus flowers and peonies that grew under trees of peach and pomegranate. A group of peacocks strutted across the tiles and the air was scented with lavender and rose.

'The flowers inspire the stone; the water mirrors the sky,' said Salek. 'Just as the garden reflects each item within itself, so the soul must find an echo with God.'

It was a sanctuary of opposites. Here was water when all around was dry; shade when all around was exposed to the sun; fruit when all around was arid; perfume when all around was stench; life when all around was death.

Beyond the formal gardens stood a meadow of wild

flowers, where young couples appeared to walk towards each other, exchange gifts, and then part. They were at such a discreet distance that Paolo asked Salek what they were doing.

'It is a place without words.'

They watched a young girl pass them amidst the grasses, picking flowers. Her long dark hair was held in a red bow, and she moved slowly, dreamily, and with such natural grace that Paolo longed to talk to her.

'Wait,' said Salek, 'her man will come. Then you will see.'

A fine-boned young boy in a white tunic arrived, carrying a small bouquet. As he lay down, the girl held out a white lotus blossom.

'You know what that means?' asked Salek. 'You understand?'

Paolo could hardly see what was happening. 'No,' he answered.

Salek continued. 'She is speaking to him. She is saying, "Am I not pretty?" Now he will pick a flower of paradise, as if to say . . .'

'You are lovelier than the flowers of paradise . . .'

'Good. You understand.'

Now the girl presented her lover with a blush rose: 'Do you love to look upon me?'

'Now look,' said Salek. 'He will give her a flower which answers her question. "As a tiger-lily loves to gaze upon its own shadow."'

The girl shredded a rosebud, pulling it apart: 'Would you die for my sake?'

The boy pulled a violet out of the grass: 'Without question, I'll submit my neck to the bowstring.'

Then the two laughed and kissed.

'You see,' explained Salek, 'love has its own language.'

But Paolo couldn't approach girls with flowers or sit quietly by and hope that one of them might kiss him. He wanted to speak to them in their own language, send them a note, or write them a poem. He knew that he should learn the flattery of flirtation, however absurd it might be. 'I love the fall of shadow on your cheek. Your eyes fragment under the sun. They are as changeable as the sea.' It sounded ridiculous, but he had seen men do this and they always seemed to be successful. Why was this? Was love no more than a game?

He tried to practise in his head as he walked: 'You have the perfect mouth,' he said aloud. 'Your walk is as beautiful as the flight of a swallow.'

'What are you saying?' asked Salek.

'Nothing,' Paolo replied.

'You must be careful,' said Jacopo sternly. 'You cannot say such things aloud. Anyone might respond.'

But Paolo began to think it hardly made any difference since these were the only two people who ever listened: an ageing Seljuk Turk and a Jewish merchant who missed his wife.

Paolo found women distant and exotic, like rare orchids, and he wondered if he would ever know them; if there would ever be a day on which his beloved would turn to him and say: 'No one has told me these things before. You alone must know my soul. Be with me now. Love me.'

Looking at his hands that night, he wondered how long it might be until he loved, or if one day he would wake and find himself too old, and that he had missed out on such companionship altogether. He tried to think if each part of his body aged at the same rate, or whether it could be out of kilter. Could a person have old hands and yet a young face? When did the body stop growing into maturity and diminish towards death? Was there a single moment, or did each part of the body reach its peak at a different age, until, finally, every muscle, bone, follicle, sinew, and blood cell came together at last, united in decline, accelerating towards a final amen?

He began to think of the oldest people he had ever seen, and those he had known who had died young. How long would he be here, on this earth, alone, with his inevitable deterioration, and how much longer might he live? How many summers? Ten? Twenty? Thirty? Or just one? How many winters? Should he really live each day as if it were his last? And if this was the day, how should he spend it?

As he inspected his body, he wondered if anyone would ever look at it in such detail. Would some tender love once know his back as well as he knew his own thumb? How much of Paolo's body would be known and loved by someone before it began to decay?

ත

Three weeks later they reached the city of Herat. It seemed to glow with the flames of small fires outside low clay dwellings and towers of beaten earth. They made their approach through an alley of dark pines where the cries of the pistachio sellers mingled with the distant sound of drumming on a *dhol*. Somewhere there must have been a wedding party. 'Khorasan is the oyster of the world,' said Salek, 'and Herat is its pearl.'

Outside the great mosque, scholars and philosophers sat discussing the essential questions of life, reassuring each other that only three kinds of men are wise: one who abandons the world before it abandons him; one who prepares his grave before he enters it; and one who has pleased the Lord before meeting him.

Salek approached the men and asked where they might find lodgings for the night. They were then directed to a small *Rabat* where several traders and travellers had already gathered, roasting lamb and drinking the first of that year's wine.

When Paolo asked about the route ahead to Badakh- shan, many of them refused to answer, convinced that an ill omen had befallen the place and they would suffer misfortune if they told any traveller where it lay. But then, at the end of the evening, the innkeeper asked Paolo to follow him across the courtyard.

'The place you seek is of infinite riches and infinite pain,' he whispered, 'and few travellers return. It is bad to speak of such a place, but this man knows. He is called Yusuf. Be patient and he will tell you.'

The man was cooking a cauldron of *khoresht*, a lamb stew with dill, coriander, dried limes, and kidney beans. Although his hair had faded and his face had wizened, Paolo could tell that the man must have been handsome in his youth, for he carried himself with pride. He wore a *muraqqa*, a patchwork coat made from ninety-nine different pieces of cloth, symbolising, so he said, all the illusions of the world, and he looked out into the distance as steam from the cauldron rose around him.

Then Paolo noticed his eyes and the stillness of his gaze.

'Are you blind?'

'The emerald loses its richness, quartz becomes pale, and silver is tarnished,' Yusuf answered. 'It is not a disaster. I live.'

'Was this a punishment?'

'Perhaps. Why have you come to this place?'

'I am looking for a blue stone.'

'You search for sapphire?'

'No. Not sapphire,' Paolo insisted. 'The stone from the mountains of Badakhshan.'

'Ah.' Yusuf paused. 'Lapis. Why do you seek it?'

'To know colour. To paint heaven.'

Yusuf leaned over the cauldron. 'Take food with me. There are bowls to the side.'

Paolo suddenly felt uneasy, frightened by the man's blindness, the blankness of his eyes.

'I once knew a woman from those mountains,' Yusuf said as he served out the food. 'At first I thought that she too might be blind, for I was told that she was forever shielding her eyes from light. But in fact she saw too well. The beauty dazzled her. Everything was too luminous, too sharp. Her world was filled with a variety of hue and tone so infinite that she could not distinguish one object from another. There was no outline, no distinction; everything carried an equal light. It made her mad to see so well.' His voice faded away. 'But what does it matter now?'

'But is it true, the story? There is a mountain of this stone?' Paolo asked.

'It is called Sar-i-Sang. But it is difficult to reach, and almost impossible to leave.'

'How can we find such a place?'

'It is a large kingdom, twelve days' journey in length. The settlements are built on sites of natural strength, and many of the mountain routes are impassable; not only for mules but also for people.'

'And where is the mountain?'

'You must follow the path of the Hari Rud River, through Jam and Chakcheran and Bamiyan. Then take the Shibar Pass before going north to Pul-i-Khumri and Taloqan. From Taloqan you must go to Faizabad.'

Yusuf stopped, and it seemed as if he was not trying to remember the route but his own youth.

'It is there?' asked Paolo.

'No. It is not there. There is a river outside Faizabad which you must forge. It is icy and fast flowing, with strong currents. Then you must ride as far as Barak. After

Barak you may have to leave your animals, but if you travel before the first snows then they may be able to take you. Choose good mules who are used to the mountains and pay whatever the men ask. If the tracks have not been swept away then you will be lucky enough.'

'And then?'

'No,' said Yusuf. 'Still you have not arrived. You must travel high into the mountains for three days and two nights. Be careful in darkness because the winds are strong, and the precipice sheer. To fall is death. But if you have survived so far then the women will come out to greet you.'

'The women?'

'You will see no men.'

'Why not?'

'Ask them. My beloved would have told you. I cannot.'

Paolo noticed that the man's blind eyes had filled with sadness. 'What happened?'

'I loved her. She died.'

'I am sorry.'

'Sometimes I think she only loved me because I could not see at all. Like the others, she saw too well.'

'And now you are alone?'

'I live only in memory.'

'And that keeps you alive?' asked Paolo.

Yusuf stood up, as if the conversation were at an end. 'We must live for love if we live at all.'

'I have not known such desire.'

'Love is not the same as desire,' Yusuf replied, 'but I

cannot tell you more until you know something of which I speak. Have you ever felt anything of love?'

'I do not see well. One day a woman might take pity on me for that, but there are times when love seems too much to hope for.'

'And will you ever see more clearly?'

Paolo thought for a moment. 'I cannot imagine such a thing. But I do want to know what it is to see into the distance and discover where I stand in the world, living life in all its fullness, able to look as others look, living with a greater knowledge of what is close and what is far, understanding what matters and what does not.'

'I am not sure you need eyes for that,' Yusuf replied.

SAR-I-SANG

They were no more than a month away from Badakhshan but it was already early autumn. Salek warned that the mountain passes would soon be frozen and blocked by snow. 'It is not good here,' he muttered. 'There is a wind that lasts one hundred and twenty days. Fully laden mules are carried away like leaves. Is stone worth death?'

Jacopo was adamant. 'We must have courage now that we have come so far.'

After two more weeks they tracked the course of the River Kokcha, fringed with willow, wild cherry, hawthorn, and poplar. At times they could trace the route of those who had gone before, following the fluffs of cotton caught on the mulberry bushes. To the south lay a range of mountains, rising in terraces and covered with dark forests. The climb became steeper, and eventually debouched onto a green plateau, where the animals could graze. A pale-blue mist hung low between the peaks, shrouding the valley and path ahead. The colours separated and reformed, as if the mountains had become a prism of quartz through which light divided and conjoined, the landscape forever recreating itself, endlessly chameleon.

Salek fretted. He told them that he had heard of a man from these parts who had made a profit by claiming that he could capture souls, stealing them from people while they were still alive. He would then either demand a ransom for their return or sell them on to criminals and sinners, terrifying his victims with the claim that they would never be able to live after death without his aid.

It was best to trust no one and move swiftly through the mountain passes, making good ground when it was possible, and sheltering at the base of the hills when it was not. Salek was adept at anticipating the weather, urging his companions to stop and settle even when they complained that the skies were clear. He knew of the winds, the speed of change, and the dangers of adventure.

Paolo wondered whether they would ever reach Badakhshan and how they could tell which of these mountains might contain the stone. He was saddle-sore, his calves and lower back ached, and he feared that his companions might turn on him at any moment, blaming him for this part of the journey.

The landscape appeared empty and foreboding, as if it had been abandoned after futile attempts to tame it long ago. Tribes of settlers had moved on, unable to find sustenance from the barren rock.

But then, just as the men began to fear that they might be lost, Salek noticed four black figures, blurred shapes on horseback, riding through the valley towards them, holding their spears aloft.

'Women,' he observed. 'All of them.'

'Are they attacking?' asked Jacopo.

'Wait.'

The women were dressed in pleated *chadri*, long ochre robes which blew back in the wind, and their legs were bound with strips of grey cloth. Blocking the path ahead, they pulled up their horses and asked the men where they meant to travel.

'East,' replied Salek. 'Through the hills.'

'Follow.'

They turned, expecting immediate obedience. The men steered their mules up through a narrow pass and approached a settlement of eight large tents at the foot of the mountain. They had been placed in front of a cave which had been crowned with antlers and god-like images wedged into the crevice of the rock. It was surely a sacred doorway, the entrance to a series of further dwellings.

Six women stood behind a row of flame, holding shallow bowls of water.

'You must pass between the fires.'

The men were shown how to purge themselves through a gate of flame, scattering water into the air as libation and obeisance to the sun and the winds. They were then led to the main tent.

'This opening faces south,' said a small woman as she folded back the entrance. 'Sit to the west.'

Paolo hardly dared believe that this might be Sar-i-Sang, the mine in the mountain, the heart of Badakh-shan. Why else would the women be so guarded and the cave so protected?

In the darkness he could make out a hearth under a smoke hole where a cauldron boiled on a trivet. The floor was covered with straw and animal skins.

'What would you have with us?' It was a woman's voice.

Salek asked if the women followed the code of the hills, giving refuge to travellers regardless of their lineage. They were tired and would be grateful for shelter.

'If you come in peace then you are welcome.'

The rest of the women began to enter the dwelling and sat on the matted floor. They seemed suspicious, as if waiting for guidance.

'What is happening?' whispered Jacopo. 'Where are the men?'

'Wait,' urged Salek.

A young girl poured mint tea into small pottery cups. As she handed the drink to the men they sat in awkward silence. Paolo looked at the group of half-veiled women. 'What do we do?' he whispered to Salek.

'We wait,' he repeated.

Salek lit his pipe. 'Who are you?' he asked.

A woman emerged from the darkness into the light. 'I am Aisha. These are my people.' She was taller and darker than the other women, and was dressed in a long ochre chador. Paolo watched as she walked towards them, slowly and gracefully, accustomed to authority and obedience.

Jacopo was unable to restrain himself. 'Where are your men? Are they hunting?'

'There are no men.'

'No men?' asked Salek and, at that moment, Paolo knew they had come to the place Yusuf had described.

'Only boys. The children that survived. This is the valley of widows.'

'There was a war?'

'Two winters ago,' the woman replied. 'This will be our third. Our only hope is for the children to grow and replace the men we have lost.'

'Why did they not take you as wives?' Salek asked.

'They took our stone. It was more precious.'

Paolo leaned forward, trying to look at Aisha more closely. He could see her dark hair fall onto her shoulders beneath the scarf.

'Those that survived swore they would return in the spring,' she continued. 'They stole our food. They killed our men. And we are all that we have left.'

'I have heard tell of this stone,' Paolo said quietly.

'It is a curse,' Aisha replied. 'No matter how far we travel with it, or wherever we hide it, we cannot escape the bloodshed it brings.'

'What happened?' asked Paolo.

'They had gunpowder. We did not. Dujan, my man,

rode into their fire. We watched from the mountain, men riding hard at each other, their swords held high, gleaming in the light of the valley.'

She paused as if this was already the end of the story.

'When they fell I could feel my own life falling. It happened so quickly and yet it is slow when I recall it. I think of it every day, and each day it lengthens. Sometimes the memory will fill an entire day and I will be able to think of nothing else. Perhaps this is what it is to grieve.'

'Please. Continue,' said Salek.

'After our enemies had left we walked through the remains of the battle. Such wounds. Bright blood against bone. Dead horses. The men were so heavy. We washed them by the waters. When they had been cleansed, we built great fires, higher than any of us had ever seen. The children gathered wood, plants, and roots, anything that they thought would burn, crying as they did so, but quietly, because they were frightened by the rage of their mothers. Some women even pulled down their homes because they could no longer see any purpose in living. They ripped them apart, piece by piece, carrying walls and roofs to the fire. Shirin, my sister, set the pyre ablaze.

'It takes so long for bodies to burn. I did not know this before. I wish I did not know it now.

'Then we mourned. We sang the songs our fathers had taught us, through the night, until the sun rose again. The pyre burned into the next day. It was only after the sun had fallen again that the fires were quiet and our men were no more. We waited until the ashes were cool.

The ash of our men and the fires in which they had burned would return to the earth.

'I took a handful and could still feel the heat in the ash, as if it were the heat of my husband against me. In the madness of grief I thought the heat was his life and that I might create him again, and I could cry out to the gods, "Make him anew! You, who made him once, make him once more. Do not leave me without such a love. You, who can shape a life and change destinies, you, who know what miracles can be, do this now for me. Turn this ash once more."

'But the gods were silent.

'And so we took the ash to the stream, handful by handful, and we let the lives of our loves fall away from us. I do not know how long this lasted. Perhaps it was night again. The stream became a river. It raged as we did. We thought we might stop it, dam it with ash, but the force of the water was strong, like blood.'

She looked at Paolo. 'It used to be sweet. But now when we drink from the stream, we know that we are drinking the water of our forefathers. We remember that day. We drink the water so that we never forget them.'

'May your men be blessed,' said Jacopo, 'and may they have found peace.'

'So this is why the stone is a burden. And if you wish to see it then you must prove worthy of it,' Aisha replied.

'We have money,' said Jacopo. 'We can trade.'

'And what if we do not want your money? What if we do not need to trade?'

'Everyone needs to trade.'

'I will decide what we need and what we do not.'

Paolo realised that even though they had arrived, the sight of the stone might yet be withheld from them.

'Now you must sleep,' Aisha was saying, suddenly distracted, 'and in the morning you must tell me why you want to see our stone. Tell us why you think you are so worthy of it.'

'It is not a question of worth,' said Jacopo.

'Do not lie to me.'

'I will tell you now,' said Paolo, but Aisha cut him short.

'In the morning. Now rest,' and as the men rose to be shown to a tent where they might sleep, she added: 'They say that some men can never love again once they have seen the blue of our stone. After the sight of the mountain their life elsewhere means nothing.'

Paolo was unafraid. 'We would see that stone.'

ಬಬ

They were shown to a small tent with simple matting on the floor. The women gave them sheepskin blankets and gestured that they should lie down. As soon as they had left, Salek told Jacopo and Paolo that even though they might be prepared to risk their lives in pursuit of the stone, he was not. 'It is too dangerous,' he insisted. 'And I do not trust them.'

'I have never bargained as that woman proposes,' said Jacopo. 'Why must we prove ourselves worthy? Why can she not trade like anyone else?'

'Because it is a treasure,' said Paolo. 'Perhaps it can only be given, never bargained.'

'Those men took it soon enough,' said Salek.

'But why have they not returned?' Paolo replied. 'Perhaps some terrible fate has befallen them.'

'Nonsense,' said Jacopo. 'It is because no one wanted to buy the stone from them. Perhaps it is only painters who want such a stone. Everyone else is content with turquoise. We should never have come.'

'We cannot stay,' said Salek.

'At least let me talk to her,' said Paolo. 'Now that we have come so far.'

'You think you can convince her?' asked Jacopo.

Salek lit a pipe. 'Perhaps we have more chance with the boy. She might pity him.'

'It is I who need the stone most. Let it be me that speaks to her,' Paolo insisted.

'First make her show it to us,' said Jacopo. 'Then we will know whether it has been worth our effort. It may have no value, and perhaps she lies.'

'I do not think so,' Paolo replied. 'I heard how Yusuf spoke of it.'

Jacopo was surprised by such boldness. 'Then you will know how hard you must try to persuade her to part with such a stone.'

೧೧

The next morning, when the men emerged from their tent, they could see that the women were up and working, preparing skins and sewing them with sinew. They were given bread and goat's milk, and then taken to the main tent to see Aisha once more.

Salek and Jacopo looked at Paolo. He paused, uncertain whether or not to tell Aisha the true nature of his journey. 'I have a friend,' he began.

Immediately Aisha interrupted. 'Man or woman?'

'A man.'

'There is no woman?'

'No.'

She seemed amused. 'Tell me of this man.'

'He is a painter in the city of Siena. I hope to take him the stone.'

'Why does he need it?'

'To turn it into paint.'

Aisha was shocked. 'You would destroy it?'

'No. He would spread it far and wide, as colour across a wall.'

'And what will your friend paint with this colour?'

'Eternity,' Paolo answered. 'A world without grief.'

'But has he seen it? How can he know?'

'He paints to take away the fear of death; to bring the consolation of a greater place beyond our own.'

'We will live on?'

'This is the belief of my people, that there is a future for our deepest loves.'

'I share that hope. But why this stone?'

'I have heard it is a colour like no other, and that with it we might paint a world like no other.'

'A noble ambition,' said Aisha doubtfully.

'Let us do so. Even if you refuse, even if you will not give it to us or trade at all, I ask you at least to let us see the stone and then depart. Then I can tell my friend that I did all that I could to complete my task. Do not let our journey be in vain.'

'And why should I trust you?'

'Because I come in peace and do not travel for myself.'

Aisha smiled sadly. 'You speak well.'

'I only speak the truth.'

Aisha said nothing. Paolo could not tell if she had suddenly changed her mind or had lost interest.

Then she spoke. 'You have come for your friend, and so I will answer in friendship. Make ready. The way is hard.'

৩৩

An hour later she appeared at their tent, and a small boy stood beside her, holding on to her skirts.

'This is Jamal,' she announced.

The boy must have been eight years old, and he appeared both sullen and mistrustful. Salek stepped forward to talk to him, but Aisha interrupted: 'He does not speak. If you wish to see the mountain, then Paolo must follow him. He will take you.'

'The entrance is not here, at the mouth of the cave?'

'No. That is our temple. The stone is hidden. I have warned that it is dangerous but Jamal climbs well. He knows the quickest path.'

Paolo looked up. He could see the steep wall above, then the rock spur below a cornice. To the right stood a snow- and ice-filled gully; to the left avalanche runnels scored the mountain.

Jamal had already begun the ascent. Paolo put his right foot in the lowest crevice, found a hand hold, and began to lever himself up. He had never climbed at such a steep angle. No step was ever certain, no hold secure. All he could do was cleave to the rock, the stone close against his face.

The altitude was such that he could hardly breathe. Paolo imagined falling and his head splitting open below. He could only survive by concentrating on the texture and detail of the mountain, its resolution and its strength: the fine cracks, the strange sheen, unexpected crevices. Looking closely, Paolo noticed that the pattern of the rock mirrored the whorl of his fingers, obscenely enlarged.

He pulled his head back to distance himself from the face, and sensed that he might fall at any moment, backwards, away from the mountain, his life disappearing into the void of winter. What would it mean if his life ended now?

At last he found himself on a high ledge where Jamal made them wait for his mother to join them. Paolo wondered if she had ascended by a different route, one that was far simpler, for when she appeared both she and the women who had accompanied her were perfectly calm. Perhaps the difficult route had been selected only to test his ability and intent?

'Jamal has brought you safely here,' said Aisha. 'Follow me.'

She led them to a small dark entrance in the rock face.

'I cannot see,' said Paolo.

'Our ancestors made a tunnel. We will need fire to travel within it.'

A woman gave Aisha a flaming brand which she passed to Paolo; others followed carrying a supply of firewood which they roped against the wall.

'The stone is hidden beneath the surface. It is the blue from which the gods moulded us. It is not of this world. We must heat the rock.'

The women felt for crevices and placed wood against the stone. Then they roped sections together as if they were making a series of giant hammocks. A flint was struck repeatedly and the wood began to catch.

The flame flared up, first gold, then blue.

The heat intensified, warming the cave, and then, just as the flames were beginning to die down, the women threw snow against the rock.

The mountain spat back at them as the fire and ice fought for control of its surface, but the women continued as if it were their enemy.

They gestured to Paolo, urging him to continue the fight, miming the way in which he should cut at the rock, pointing to the most vulnerable sections of the surface. One of them handed him a pickaxe.

'Strike,' ordered Aisha. 'It cracks under heat and snow.'

Paolo swung but his pick bounced off the rock, vibrating its energy back into his hand.

'Harder.'

Paolo thought that the mountain must be as impenetrable as when he had climbed it, but he was now determined to reveal its secret. He began to strike blow after blow as Aisha prised stone out with her fingers, breaking her nails, reaching into each fissure.

Then she picked up a rock and hammered at the sides of the cave, following each crack and crevice: stone against stone.

The lapis fell to the floor.

Aisha bent down, picked out a piece of stone, and handed it to him. It was jagged and cold, but a strange heat emerged from its centre. 'Take it outside.'

On one side the stone was awkward mountain rock, but on the reverse, the side that had been newly cut, Paolo saw an intense irradiated blue, pitted with gold and streaked with silver.

He had thought that he knew stone, and could no longer be surprised by the way in which gold could be threaded, or silver glisten within. Other men might want to separate the blue from the white, or extract the gold and silver and sell it. They might even discard the blue of the lapis lazuli that he held in his hand.

But now he understood why he had come. Once he had known the richness of sapphire, so translucent that it had almost been white. He had seen the paleness of aquamarine, witnessed the play of pearl in precious opal, and admired the deep-blue gleam in the midst of a piece of firestone. He had once seen a blue so dark as to be black, splintered in tourmaline, disseminated in the darkness of chromite, weathered in the verdigris of caledonite. He had seen it shining as silver in hematite and pyrite, and in galena and in quartz. He had inspected the brittle blue of antimony, and the soft blue of stephanite. He had found a fine blue in the poisonous crystals of cyanite and amidst the white of arsenic. He had seen it in needle-shaped crystals, in druses: granular blues, scaly blues, massive, efflorescent, spathic, and fibrous. He had found blue in rock salt, in quartz, and even in topaz. He had seen pearls that were blue, and had once examined an emerald striated with a strange intrusive rivulet of azure. He knew the heat of blue flame and the cold metallic blue found in the gills of fish or deep in the ice. But he had never seen a colour such as this.

He held the stone in his hand, glowing as if lit by its own light, carved from the sky. All the blue that there had ever been in the world now seemed concentrated in this rock.

He heard Aisha's voice. 'People who come tell us that they have never known such beauty,' she said.

'They are right,' said Paolo.

She stood close to him. 'And we tell them in turn that we have never seen so much death.'

'Why?'

'The feathers of the peacock are its enemy. There are some who say that we must take this stone to the ends of the world. Then, when we have journeyed further than any who have travelled before, we must throw it into the darkness that takes all life. Only then will we be free.'

She turned the stone in Paolo's hands. 'Look into its veins. What do you see?'

'Azure. Cobalt. Violet. It changes in the light. Perhaps it is the colour of the night sky.'

'And can you see between the colours?'

'Where?'

She took his hand and ran her finger across the stone. 'Can you not tell that another colour lies here, along this vein?'

Paolo leaned towards her. The stone followed the curve of her hand.

'Some men cannot see it.'

Paolo could sense her breath in the cold air. 'What colour do you mean?'

She pointed to a strand of azure. 'Perhaps you are like my son.'

The boy was watching them.

'He cannot see into the distance?' asked Paolo.

'No. He cannot tell colour: red from green, mulberries from their leaves. Everything is tone and shade; he cannot describe what he sees. Perhaps it is a punishment because I see so clearly.'

'But he cannot speak?'

'He can speak. He chooses not to.'

'How long has he been like this?'

'Since the day they came.'

Jamal began to pull at her side. It had started to rain. Aisha ushered the boy back into the shelter of the cave.

Paolo looked out from the mountain, down to the river and over to the hills beyond. So, he thought, it is for this that I have travelled.

He tried to imagine the stone as paint, the wash of colour on walls, infinite space.

Then he felt Aisha beside him once more.

'Look at the light, over there, in the distance through the rain: the arc that hangs in the sky. What are the colours that you see?'

'A dark blue at the base, a strange green, orange, pale gold.'

'You do not see the violet next to the blue at the base? Or the colour between the orange and the gold?'

'It is all one.'

'You must learn to look between the colours. Can you see the lavender band?'

'Show me,' said Paolo.

Aisha pointed. 'Look. And there, beyond, can you see the fainter and fainter repeats of the main bow, the arch of purple, the strongest green?'

'I can only see the main arc, vague in the distance,' Paolo apologised. 'I see sharply only when objects are near.'

'Then we are opposite,' Aisha replied. 'I prefer distance. The weight of close colour is too strong.'

They stood watching the rainbow. Paolo thought it

looked like an upturned bowl of cloud. 'Will you see your husband again?' he asked. 'In another life?'

'I have learned not to expect such things.' She looked up and noticed that Paolo was staring at the nape of her neck. The fall of her hair. 'How old are you?' she asked.

Paolo blushed. 'I am seventeen. I do not know.'

'Then you must tell me of your life. It is, I think, your turn.'

ಬಲ

That evening, after Paolo had told his companions of the day's events, Salek seemed almost cheerful. 'You have spoken well and worked hard, Paolo. Now there is only one thing left for you to do.'

'Don't tease him,' Jacopo interrupted. 'The boy is still young.'

'No, no, no,' Salek insisted. 'It is time. He is old enough.'

'For what?' Paolo asked.

'You know perfectly well,' said Salek. 'It is what you have been waiting for.'

'Don't be foolish.'

'I am not. I know women. I have seen the way she is with you.'

'She pities me.'

'No, she does not. You have crossed the world to find what your friend needs most. What might you do for her?'

'Leave him,' said Jacopo.

Paolo thought he had only been excited by the stone; now he wondered if all his nervousness on the journey had been but the anticipation of love.

That night he dreamed that he was trapped inside the mountain. He was surrounded by blue, by shadow, and by darkness. He could not see the ground underneath him or the route ahead, and walked with arms outstretched, as if blind, trying to find a tunnel that would lead him back into the light. He could hear voices in the distance, women laughing, and a great gathering sweep of sound as snow slid down from the rocks above. At the same time the uneven floor of the cave began to give way beneath his feet. To move in any direction meant darkness and danger, and yet he knew that he could not keep still, that he would have to search for a way out.

Blue flares illuminated parts of his path and led him into the light between shadows. As he made his way south Paolo began to see shapes, different forms, all in one colour, bleeding into each other so seamlessly that it was almost impossible to distinguish the nature of objects. At one point he thought he could see Simone, painting the walls of the cave by the light of a fire, complaining that he did not have enough pigment. It would be exhausted before he had finished the sky.

In another false opening, Salek reached out to him, his arm discoloured by a livid blue bruise. He was trying to guide him out of the cave, but just as Paolo attempted to hold on to his arm, the figure vanished, and he found himself alone once more, his path blocked by rock.

Women in the distance appeared to beckon him forward but Paolo knew that it must surely be a mirage, a dream within a dream from which he could not wake. He tried to cry out, find help, or rouse himself from the dream, but no sound came from his mouth. The back of his throat had been sealed.

Then he saw Aisha in a gown so pale that it was almost white. She was walking towards him, and yet, at the same time, she gained no distance. She was eternally out of reach, holding the lapis lazuli in her outstretched arms, saying: 'The colour of heaven. The blood of angels.' The light increased in intensity until it was almost dazzling, shining directly at Paolo.

He raised his hands, clasping them against his eyes, feeling the heat burn on his fingers, and then staggered forward, for he knew that he could not stop. He had to escape the cave and flee from this dream.

Then he felt the ground change, the whiteness soften, and the air cool. Before him, outside the cave, across a stretch of pebbled shore, he saw a turquoise ocean and an azure sky. He ran towards the sea, his bare feet slipping on the stones. But as he ran, the tide appeared to ebb at the same rate, and he knew that he could never reach the water's edge. The faster he ran the more the tide receded, further and further from his grasp.

A terrible heat burned through his body. He looked up for the sun, to see where this sudden warmth had come from, but it surged at him from all sides. The temperature rose so fast that he could no longer move. His only hope of calm lay either in the distant sea ahead or amidst the cool pebbles beneath his feet.

He longed to fall but his body would not obey. All he had to do was to let his knees give, but they did not move. He looked down, and found that the whole of his body apart from his head and his arms had now become as rock and that he was as blue and as solid as the mountain.

How could he turn himself back into flesh? The only way in which he could reach the ground would be to cut away at his own body, to chisel and to hammer just as they had struck at the mountain. He would have to destroy himself.

Perhaps these rocks and pebbles were the remains of all the men before him who had tried to gain access to the secrets of the mountain.

Now Paolo began to punch himself, hurting his hands on the rock of his body. He looked at his arms, the only flesh he could see. How could they compete with the stone?

As he struck out he noticed that the blood across his knuckles was blue. He watched it seep from his hands and drip onto the ground, wondering how much blood he had left. Then he felt his body surge and fall forwards, his face thrown against cold stone.

He sensed the sharpness of oblivion, and death no longer worried him. There would be no one to trouble him any more, no orders to take. He would fall into the dark-blue sleep of forgetfulness.

He rested and waited, listening to his own breathing. At last he became aware of a presence, a figure lying beside him. Paolo opened his eyes and saw a woman's arm, coloured with the lead blue of flesh before death.

He pressed down onto the large smooth pebbles, raising himself to see the pale form on the shore.

It was his mother.

ನಿನ್

When Paolo woke he did not believe he had done so. He had long known not to rely on his sight, but now he doubted if he could trust his thoughts.

Later that morning he followed Jamal up the mountain once more to work amidst the women, heating, freezing, and striking the rock. As he climbed he found that he could not stop thinking of Aisha. He wanted to see her again, and when they reached the summit he kept looking round, hoping that she might be near. If her son would only speak then he could have asked him where she was or followed him to her, but Jamal seemed only interested in watching his visitor work.

At times the boy stood too close, irritating in his proximity, and appeared to be judging Paolo's ability to strike at the rock. At one point he was almost hit by the swing of the pick.

'Step back,' Paolo snapped.

Jamal looked at him with curiosity, surprised by

this loss of temper. He moved away, and then returned within minutes to stand as close as he had done before, deliberately defiant. There was a stubborn determination in his eyes and Paolo recognised that his father must have been the same. It was a look that claimed the land.

Paolo returned to work. The rock split under the weight of his attack, but the vibration surged back into his hands. He dropped the pickaxe and closed his eyes. Debris collapsed around him. Dust, rock, and powder cascaded into his hair and onto his face. When he opened his eyes to find his bearings, another spattering of dust dropped into his right eye.

He turned away from the rock face and smarted, walking out of the cave and into the light, raising his hand to extract the dust.

Then he heard Aisha's voice. 'Wait.'

He half opened his left eye as the right screwed up in pain. He could just see her lifting the edge of her blouse up to her lips. She folded a piece over into a thin strip and wet it with her tongue.

'Here. Let me. Close your eyes.'

He felt the cloth against his eyes, brushing the dust clear.

A piece of grit had lodged on the side of his nose and Aisha blew the speck away. 'There.'

Paolo rubbed at his eyes and opened them. He saw her face close to his, the pores of her skin. Quickly, briefly, she stroked his cheek. As he felt the tenderness of her touch he noticed the blue of the stone underneath her fingernails.

She smiled and stepped back. 'You have done well.'

'I have worked hard.'

'Then you must be rewarded.' Aisha reached into a sack and picked out a stone. 'Here. Take it.'

Paolo held out his hand and she placed the lapis in his palm. It was paler in the bright light of the afternoon, half bleached by the sun. 'I hope your friend in Siena will be happy.'

Paolo looked back at the mountain. 'I can hardly believe I am here. It is like a dream.'

'No. It is no dream. This is the life we have.'

The air was colder, and Jamal came and stood by his mother's side, his presence suggesting that they make their descent before the evening mist and darkness. Aisha nodded, and adjusted her headscarf, wrapping herself against the cold. They took the longer, shallower path, and Paolo swung his sack over his shoulder before steadying himself for the route ahead. They walked in silence, concentrating on keeping their balance. Mother and son held on to each other as their guest followed behind. Only when the ground became even did he speak again.

'There is something I would like to ask,' Paolo began.

Aisha let go of Jamal's hand and let him run ahead. 'Which is?'

'I would like to know why you have been so kind.'

'You need to know?' She was almost amused.

'I do not need to know. I want to know. I am not certain why. Perhaps you can teach me.'

'I have nothing to teach. Perhaps you should not ask. I might change my mind.' She smiled.

'Do not do that.'

They were nearing the settlement, and the women who had stayed behind were preparing a broth of chicken over a simple fire.

'It is hard,' she began, 'but I think I am weary. Tired of defending such a mountain. We should move on to new lands, fresh hunting grounds. We stay here in memory of our men, but it is too painful. Perhaps if we give the stone away, we might redeem the past.'

'I am not sure I understand.'

'Perhaps you do not need to. Only make sure your friend paints well. Another life. A better life. I would see such a world.'

ณณ

By the time Paolo returned to the tent, his hands and his cheeks had frozen. He hoped that Salek and Jacopo had prepared a fire.

As he thought about his two companions he realised that he had almost started to resent the time they spent in prayer rather than in practicalities. At least Salek always checked the mules and the safety of their possessions but Jacopo appeared to do little apart from pray and watch other people work.

Paolo pulled back the flap and entered their dwelling,

lowering his bag and tools gently to the floor. 'Look,' he said. He opened his sack and placed a large piece of lapis on the floor.

Jacopo was drinking tea and appeared unsurprised. 'How much will she give us?'

Paolo could not believe that this was all Jacopo appeared to care about. 'I do not know. As much as we can carry.'

'Then we must start, and work quickly,' said Salek. 'If we stay too long we will be trapped here for the winter. The mountains will be impassable. We must prepare to leave.'

'But we have only just arrived.' Paolo thought what staying for the winter might mean. Shelter, warmth, and Aisha. Perhaps he should cut the stone more slowly. 'We need enough for two mules.'

'One mule,' argued Salek.

'It is a big wall for Simone to paint,' Paolo insisted. 'And there will be other frescoes. We can sell to other painters.'

'Will she give it to you if she knows you are so keen to sell it? Has it not been given in friendship?'

'It has.'

'Then stay in friendship,' said Salek. 'And talk with her once more. Perhaps we should leave you alone.'

Paolo felt himself blush.

'You must be wary of widows,' Jacopo said ominously, 'especially those who are still young.'

'I do not know why you are telling me this,' Paolo

answered and sat down by the fire. 'Nothing has happened.'

'She is older than you,' said Jacopo. 'And she loves the man she has lost. There will be none like him. The worst that can happen has happened. Having lost everything she can now lose nothing.'

'I think she has hope.'

'And I think she has not. She does not mind if she dies now or tomorrow. She can risk anything or everything. This makes her dangerous.'

'Dangerous?'

'She has suffered. Now she will want revenge: against the world, men, fate, and destiny. Perhaps even you . . .'

ᱬ

The next morning Paolo found the excuse he needed to see Aisha once more. Although he could imagine how the stone might become paint, he asked if he could see how the lapis changed when it was cut, ground, or polished. He wanted to watch her make articles of trade: rings, brooches, jewels, and amulets.

'If you help me,' she answered, 'then I will show you.'

She sat at a low wooden table, chipping away with a small iron hammer, and then trimmed the edges to create the oval shape for a brooch. 'Now,' she said, 'I am going to put the stone in the vice. Pass me the saw.'

Paolo watched her lean forward and cut away at the lapis. Then she ground the surface to remove any burs.

'I need a pan of grit and water,' she said. 'It is there.'

Paolo poured water and coarse sand into the pan.

'Remember the lid.'

Aisha tipped the stone into the container, and sealed it. 'Now shake the stone, washing and grinding it down.'

Paolo began to shake the pan vigorously.

'No.' She stopped him. 'Gently. It takes time. Rock the stone against the sand. Imagine you are searching for gold with a sieve.'

'I have never done such a thing.'

'Here,' she said, taking the pan from his hands. 'Let me show you.'

She began to rock and tilt the mixture. Paolo listened to the sound of the stone against the sand and watched the light fall on her hands. He looked once more at her eyes and thought how swiftly they could move between joy and sadness. They could gleam and they could darken. Even her laugh was underpinned with pain, as if it should have lasted longer and could never quite finish, dying before it had reached its height.

'Now you.'

Paolo took the pan and began to rock the lapis against the sand once more.

'Better. We must take great care.' Aisha was almost amused by Paolo's attempts to refine the stone. 'I would have thought that you, knowing of glass, would see how fragile the world can be.'

'Not stone.'

'It can crack as easily as glass. It has flaws.'

'In Venice there is a special glass which shatters if any trace of poison touches it.'

'You poison each other in Venice?'

'Every day.'

She laughed once more.

'I would like to know as that glass knows,' said Paolo. 'To be able to tell, immediately, if things are wrong. To trust. To know where I am going. To believe the ground beneath my feet will hold me. That I will not stumble or fall.'

Aisha decanted the mixture and dried the piece of lapis in a cloth. Then she sat down and began to polish the stone. 'If you had known tragedy, then you would expect disaster and lose such fear. Live as if you were already dead.'

'Is that what you do?'

'When you have known the worst there can be no worse.'

'But I do not know what it can be like to live without fear.'

Aisha blew the dust away from the polished stone and began to carve into its surface, decorating the brooch with the shape of a phoenix. 'You are so young.'

'And you think that you are old?'

'Of course. Older than you.'

Paolo noticed that when she lowered her head to concentrate, her dark hair fell forward onto her hands. She had to stop, momentarily, brushing it back across her shoulders. It was one movement, made without interrupting her concentration, as if she were quite alone.

Paolo watched the glint of the incising tool, held firmly between her fingers, moving against the blue stone.

'There.' Aisha looked up and seemed surprised that Paolo was still in the room. She observed him strangely, tilting her head in the light. Paolo wondered if he had done anything wrong.

'Your beard,' she said, as if she had not noticed it before. 'Do you think it suits you?'

'Why do you ask?'

'Because I think you would look better without it.'

'All men have beards. Jacopo told me.'

Aisha took the mention of Jacopo's name as a challenge. 'I would like to see you without one.'

'You would not mind?'

'No. I would help you.'

'Remove it? You know how?'

'I learned to shave my father when he was old. I know how to do it.'

'I am not sure that I want to be clean shaven.'

'No? Be brave. Live boldly.'

Paolo smiled. 'There must be more to it than shaving.'

'But it's a beginning,' Aisha replied. 'Have courage.'

'How can I argue with you?' Paolo answered.

'I am sure you can learn.'

The next morning she took Paolo down to the river and told him to wash his face and wet his beard. She lit a fire, and warmed a bowl of water and wet tallow soap, rubbing the lather between her hands. Then she began to pat it gently against his face.

'Not too cold?' she asked.

She pulled her father's knife from her belt, and sharpened it on a flint from the ground.

Paolo wondered if she had ever killed a man.

'Trust me.' She smiled. 'Close your eyes.'

She stood behind him and began to shave underneath his chin, stroking the hair upwards, tilting Paolo's head in the cup of her hands.

He felt the sharpness of the blade raze through the hair of his beard, the cold air freshen against his newly exposed flesh, the back of her hand against his face.

Then he tilted his head back and felt it rest against her breasts. Aisha moved round to face him. She smiled, and he blushed as she did so, as if they both acknowledged that his last movement had not been an accident, that all he had wanted was to leave his head against her.

She began to shave his cheeks, stroking the hair downwards, and then dabbed the soap away with a cloth.

Paolo felt the cold air on his face, the warmth of the water, and the softness of her breath. He closed his eyes, letting her guide his face in her hands, breathing in the scent of almond and rosewater.

Aisha washed the knife, and then dried it on her skirts, before beginning again on his left cheek. 'What do you hope for,' she asked, 'in your life?'

'It is too much, I think.'

'Tell me. Open your eyes.'

She met his look and would not continue shaving until he spoke.

'No,' he said, 'I cannot.'

'Tell.'

'I want to look at you. Like this. Now.'

'Then look.'

'When I look closely I see with a terrible sharpness.'
She leaned back. 'Even my flaws. I must be careful.'

'You have no flaws,' he answered seriously.

'Now you flatter me. I think you should look again.'

'I am looking,' he said.

'And what do you see?'

'I see the fall of your hair against your neck, and the way it curls like a wave. I see that your eyes are not always the deepest amber, but can even become a dark green, opalescent, always changing, and that I would have to spend many hours looking into each one if I were ever to be able to describe their true colour.'

Aisha stopped. Only then did she realise how serious he had become. She threw him the cloth. 'Tell me more stories. Let me hear your voice.'

Paolo dried the rest of his face. 'I do not know what to say.'

She sat down beside him. 'Tell me anything.'

'There was a man,' he began, uncertain where his story might lead, 'who was afraid. He was so afraid that he was even scared of happiness, because he knew it would always have to end. He set sail on a journey, over the seas and across the world, hoping to lose this fear. He carried it like a bundle on his back. Everywhere he went he would open the bundle and show it to the people he met. At first he tried to sell it. Who will buy my fear? I ask for only five silver coins. But no one wanted to make such a purchase, even in order to give it to their enemies. So the man reduced the price to three silver coins, then two, then one. Still no one wanted the bundle of his fears. Then he tried to give it away. Again, he had no success. But one day, towards the end of his journey, he thought that he would leave it behind, hide it somewhere. And so he came to a cave high up in the mountains. And in the middle of the cave was a woman. He opened the bundle and showed it to her. And the woman took out the fear and looked at it. "You call this fear?" she asked. "This is nothing." And suddenly the fear was gone, cast out into the winds.'

Aisha looked straight into his eyes. 'And what happened then?'

'She began to fill the bundle with stone. It was the most beautiful stone he had ever seen. But it was also the heaviest. So, when he picked up his bundle to leave, he found that it was too heavy for him to carry. He was trapped.'

'And was he happy?'

'He had never been happier.'

'And how did they live?'

'Together, of course.'

For a while they were silent. 'If only life were such a fable,' Aisha said quietly.

'Perhaps you have listened to the wrong stories,' Paolo replied.

'Or lived the wrong life. Come. It's cold. I'm hungry. We must go back.'

᯾

That night in the men's tent Jacopo questioned the wisdom of Paolo shaving his beard. Was this love or youthful defiance?

'Have a smoke at my pipe,' said Salek. 'Now that you are a man.'

Jacopo chuckled.

'There is no need to tease me,' Paolo protested.

'Do not be angry,' said Salek. 'You should thank us. We left you alone.' He turned to Jacopo and added darkly, 'Together.'

Both men laughed, as if the word 'together' had never been more amusing. 'She misses the company of men,' Jacopo observed. 'And you have been good to her.'

'But how good?' Salek could not help adding.

'That's enough,' said Paolo testily and the men then sat in silence. Salek took out his pipe and Jacopo prepared to pray. They could hear the mules stamping their feet in the cold outside, the cry of a wolf in the distance, and a woman singing her children to sleep.

'Why do you like her so much?' asked Salek.

Paolo could not think how to answer. 'I do not know. Her presence. Her eyes,' he said simply.

'Describe them.'

Paolo thought for a moment. 'They are the deepest amber, as variable and as uncertain.'

'What kind of amber?'

'Like the heart of a fire as it gradually dies.'

'And how does the right eye differ from the left?'

'I have only looked clearly into her right eye, the side nearest to me.'

'Some would say that you had only looked into half of her soul.'

'This is only her physical appearance. There is more to her than what I see. And you know too that my sight is bad.'

'But you think that you love her?' Salek asked.

'I do not know. All I do know is that I can think only of her. Is that love?'

Jacopo returned from his prayers. 'You wish that we tell you now, in this cold?'

'Yes.'

'Of which love do you wish me to speak? The love of God for us or our love for God? The love of a father for his son, a mother for a daughter? The love of a child? The love of a husband? The love of a wife? Each is different.'

'The love of another. A man and a woman.'

'A man and a woman.'

'You and Sofia.'

'That is for us alone.'

'Do you think of Sofia all the time?'

'No, but she is always with me. I hear her voice.'

'And what does she say?'

'I talk with her. And she consoles me. I think

sometimes that if I have this love in the world then nothing else matters. There can be sadness, there can be tragedy, but all that counts is this love.'

'Then why do you travel?'

'Sometimes I love her more when we are apart. When I live with her all the time it is more difficult. Our love is kept by distance.'

'And you trust her?'

'Of course I trust her. You insult me to ask such a question.'

'And she trusts you?'

'Does it look as if I stray like a dog?'

'No.'

'Then don't ask me. What's happened to you? You think you love her, this widow?'

'I don't know. Perhaps. I cannot understand her.'

'No. But perhaps she cannot understand you. A young Italian boy . . .'

'And she is older, I know. But I feel safe.'

'Safe?'

'You mean love should be more than safety?' Paolo asked.

'I think so,' Jacopo replied.

'All I know is that I can see only her. In my thoughts and my dreams.'

'Only her?'

'She is all I care about.'

'Describe her voice to me.'

'Why?'

'Just describe it.'

'I don't understand.'

'I would like to hear what you have to say,' said Jacopo firmly.

Paolo thought, and tried to remember the last words she had said to him. *If only life were such a fable . . .* 'It is like a song that I have always wanted to hear.'

'And is it the last voice?'

'What do you mean?'

Jacopo took a long, slow breath. 'You want me to tell you of love?'

'I do.'

'Then imagine that you are dying.'

'Here?'

'I will make it easier for you. You are on a bed, not in battle, or at sea, or at the bottom of this mountain. You are comfortable, but you are weak. There is a goblet of water by your side, made from Venetian glass. You are not hungry. And there are no distractions. To have such concerns would be futile; for you know that you are going to die. You are waiting for it quite calmly: the last darkness, the final silence.

'And as you wait, in the dim of the evening, warmed by the last of the sun, you become aware of a person lying down beside you, hushing you to sleep. But who is this person? What do they say?

'You know at that moment that this is the last voice that you will hear on earth. The final farewell. You will die with this voice telling you how much you have been loved, whispering goodbye. But whose is the last voice? Would you like it to be hers?'

'I do not know.'

'Think. Imagine. Now you are lying there. Can you hear her voice?'

If only life were such a fable.

'Or is it the voice of your mother?'

I have done all that I can. I have not lived for myself, but only through you. I wanted to do this. I wanted to love.

'I cannot hear clearly. There are too many voices.'

'Then listen harder.'

You think you love her, this widow?

'I can only hear your voice. I can only imagine yours.'

'I am flattered.'

'I want it to be hers. To feel her lying down beside me. For her to be with me, just as I would be with her, now, if I had to do such a thing. I would go to her. I would listen to her breathing. I would breathe at the same rate, as if my breathing could become hers so that she should live and I might die.'

'And would you cease your travels, stay here and never leave? Give up everything?'

'Yes.'

'Never return to Simone, see Venice or your mother?'

'Perhaps my mother is already dead.'

'I do not believe you think this.'

Paolo thought what it might mean to leave and what

it might be like to stay. 'And you? Whose is the last voice you would choose to hear?'

'You ask me a question to which you must already know the answer.'

'This is true. But I want you to say it. Tell me.'

'Why, the voice of my wife, my beloved, my Sofia, crying across the wilderness,' Jacopo replied.

༄

Before Paolo slept he tried to remember the way in which Aisha looked at him. If only he could find a piece of amber that would match the beauty of her eyes and live on after her death.

Her death? Why had he imagined such a thing, now, as if he were half in love with the idea? Perhaps it was because he would then have experienced suffering, and those who knew him well would learn how much he had loved. Through his bereavement he would demonstrate that his love was greater, truer, more passionate than anything his companions had ever felt.

'Are you awake?'

It was Salek.

'Still thinking of her?'

'I am.'

'Then go to her.'

'I do not dare.'

'Love her. It is what I would do.'

'I am not you.'

'Go.' Salek turned as if to sleep. 'Tell her.'

Paolo tried to ignore him but could not stop thinking. He did not want to sleep lest he dreamed. He felt the fragility of the earth underneath him, as if it might give way at any moment. Then he tried to imagine how high the sky must be above him. He lived in a chasm of air between earth and heaven of which he could make no sense, in which he was lost.

And then he decided.

He would tell her now.

༄

He stood in the main tent watching Aisha as she slept, her long dark hair falling against her back. For a moment Paolo wanted nothing to change, for him to stay here, looking. Then she stirred. And in that instant, even though she could not yet know that Paolo was in the room, he already sensed that he should leave.

But he could not do so.

He approached the bed, sat on its edge, and lay down beside her. He listened to the wind outside and to the rise and fall of her breathing. He tried to breathe at the same rate. Perhaps he could stay here in her bed for ever, without her even knowing. He tried to think how long it would be until dawn.

But then Aisha woke with a start, frightened, half asleep, confused. 'You.'

'Yes.'

'What are you doing? Here in my bed?' She turned onto her side and smiled.

Even in the darkness, Paolo could tell that it was a smile of pity: the smile of a mother.

At once he knew that his cause was lost; before she said anything more, before she reached out to stroke his cheek or brush the hair from her eyes, he knew that he should be anywhere other than here, that he had made a mistake.

'Jamal is sleeping,' she whispered.

'I wanted to see you,' said Paolo.

Aisha smiled. 'I am sorry.'

'Why?' he asked, still hoping that he was wrong, that she would take him to her.

'No,' she said. 'I am too sad for you. I have much that is past. You are still young.'

She took him in her arms, and they held each other. Paolo buried himself in her, and she gathered him to her, but not in the way that he wanted. She cradled him as a mother cradles a boy.

He began to cry and hated himself for doing so. He could do nothing to stop it, as if he had been waiting for this moment throughout his journey. He cried for his life and for her pity; for being in her arms, for her love. And he cried for his own foolishness and stupidity; for his own youth, which, it seemed, he could never escape.

When would he ever be old enough for desire to be realised, passion felt? How long must he wait?

And then, since he must still be a boy, he felt the years slip backwards into his childhood. He cried for his mother, for her arms around him, and for safety; for a love that was unswerving, a love that he could trust for ever, and which would never let him down. He cried for the distance between them. He thought of home, the streets, the people, and the glass. The roads he knew. The church of San Donato. He cried for the laughter of his friends, and even for his father, shaping the glass in the fire. He cried for the fact that this journey might never end. And then he cried for her, for Aisha, for her life, and for her tragedy, a story he could not change or redeem, that he could neither heal nor comfort.

'My brave boy,' she said.

Later that night, after he had left Aisha, Paolo saw Salek leaving another tent, looking almost secretive. He could not understand it.

'What have you been doing?'

'Nothing.' His guide smiled. 'Like you, I have found a friend.'

'You have been very quiet about it.'

'Of course. I do not need to tell the world.'

'Is that what I have done?'

'You have been a boy. Perhaps you should try to become a man.'

'And what does that mean?' asked Paolo.

'Patience. Restraint. Calmness and strength.'

'Is that all?' Paolo replied.

When Aisha saw Paolo the next morning she was guarded, as if she had made up her mind that both their love and their friendship could have no future.

'You are distracted by the stone and by me,' she told Paolo. 'Do you ever stop to think what our life here is like? It is survival. Shelter, Food, Birth, Death. Love is a luxury. We do not expect it. And it does not come twice. Your life is privilege, adventure. You go where you will. I cannot.'

'Come with me then.'

'No. These are my people. And there is my son. Do not think you can arrive and change my life.'

'I am not asking you to do such a thing. I only wanted to be with you.'

'But how? You must return. If you stayed then you would realise how difficult our life can be. Teaching Jamal, slaughtering animals, living in cold and poverty. You have no knowledge of these things.'

'I have travelled the world.'

'And always moved on. For how long have you stopped? Never. You do not know what it is to live here. How can I ask you to do this?'

It was the first time she had acknowledged that she had even imagined a future life with him.

'Try,' Paolo replied. 'Ask me.'

'You must tell me,' she replied. 'Show me how such a thing may be possible.'

'I can only do so by loving you.'

'And how will you do that?'

'By thinking only of you. By caring for both you and your son. By promising to return, and never leaving when I have done so.'

'I don't believe you.'

'You must.'

'Why?'

Paolo leaned forward and kissed her. He closed his eyes, unable to believe either his daring or her response. So, he thought, this is what it is to begin.

His head filled with darkness.

Then gently she pushed him back.

Jamal had been watching.

ನು

Now Paolo became obsessed with the idea that Aisha's feelings were perhaps no more than pity. She looked upon him as another son. He was in a competition with Jamal that he could never win.

He watched the boy gathering stones by the river, picking them out, inspecting each one for size and shape, colour and smoothness. This then was his challenge: to love the boy who would not be loved. And how could he love him when the boy fell so short of his love for her? What was it to love another man's child?

He remembered that this was what Marco and Teresa had done. He must learn to love as they had loved.

He sat beside Jamal and helped him to sort the stone. As he did so, Paolo suddenly imagined Aisha making love to the boy's father. He tried to bury the thought back inside him, the jealousy and lust. That love was past, he knew, but yet it was ever present. The boy was testament to the fact.

How would he ever be able to match that passion? How could he replace it or redeem it? What was it to love someone who had already been loved? How could he make Aisha's life anew? And how could he think that he could ever be a father to this boy?

They began to divide the pieces of stone Jamal had collected from the river into tone and hue, light and dark. As they did so, Paolo realised that the boy was like him. He too had been alone, shy, and awkward. He too had avoided people, thinking only of pattern and of stone, hard to love.

Hard to love. That is what I am, Paolo thought. I once heard Marco say so. That is what I must be. I am lucky that anyone takes any interest in me at all. I should help this boy in his loneliness because I know what it is like to feel abandoned. We will be fatherless together.

They separated the stone.

Perhaps I could be an elder brother, Paolo thought. A brother who knew what it was like not to see well; a sibling who could protect him. And through his concern for the boy he might win the love of his mother. But could he really love the boy who was not his, or would he have to pretend? And if he did so, Aisha would surely be able to tell. He could make people believe that a piece of glass was a jewel, but how could he counterfeit love for a child?

Paolo drew a circle in the ground. Then he placed the darkest blue stone in the centre. They would create a pattern together and it would radiate colour, moving from the darkness at the centre out to the palest lapis lazuli on the outer rim. He wanted the boy to understand the depth and detail of the blue that Aisha saw: azure and cerulean, cobalt, sapphire, royal, navy, and marine; the reddish blue in damson and madder; the greenish blue of beryl, turquoise, and aquamarine; blue ash, lake, and indigo.

As they worked Paolo noticed that Jamal could tell depth and tone with astonishing clarity. The circle contained the subtlest variation, each stone shading into another. He smiled and pointed up at the sky and then back down to the earth, the blue circle above and below them.

'What are you doing?' It was Aisha's voice.

Paolo turned to see her, standing against the sun. 'We have been working.'

'Together?'

'Why not?'

Jamal ran to his mother. 'My brave boy.' She smiled, taking him into her arms.

The same words. Paolo felt the surge of jealousy and hopelessness once more. He looked at the way in which her son clung to the folds of Aisha's skirts, his head against her waist.

Now, every time Paolo saw Aisha, Jamal was there. When the boy was not standing by his mother's side, or even between them, he was never far away, like a guard who never left his watch. The more Paolo tried to ignore him, the more interesting Jamal seemed to find him. The boy never wearied. And every time Aisha spoke either of the past or her future life she would talk of her son, defensively and with pride. 'Do not be angry with his silence,' she urged.

'I am not,' Paolo lied.

'He has closed his heart, and so his mouth is silent.'

'Will he ever speak again?'

'I do not know. Every time I see him, every time he clings to me, I am reminded of what I have lost. Sometimes it hurts to have him near me, but I will never be without him. I would die rather than lose him. I have to show all who know me that love is stronger than death; that I will keep him safe, and no harm will come.'

လွ

When Aisha settled her son the following night, he looked up and said simply, 'You love him more than me.'

'No, Jamal, I don't.'

'You do.'

'I love him differently.'

'Then you admit that you love him.'

'I didn't mean to say love,' she replied.

လွ

Aisha tried to stop thinking about Paolo. It was absurd. But as she cut away at the stone she found that she could not concentrate. She kept hearing his voice and remembering the way in which he looked at her.

He had a dedication and a steadiness that appeared unshakeable. Perhaps it was because he could see so little of the world beyond himself that he knew the immediate world far better: the world of thought and emotion rather than distance and action. But what was he really like? And why did he love her?

As she made an incision into a piece of lapis, the knife slipped and cut into her left hand. Drops of blood fell onto the stone, dark red against the blue. Despite the pain, she stopped and looked at the wound, watching the blood fall, unable to believe that she had been so careless. She stood up and looked round for cloth with which to bandage her hand. There was none.

The cut was slight but deep, and she pressed her right hand over the wound. She would have to consult her sister.

'What's wrong?' Shirin asked.

'I have been careless.'

'You never cut yourself,' her sister replied.

'Now I have.'

'Here,' said Shirin. 'Let me look.' She took a cloth and dipped it in a pail of water, and then dabbed away at the cut. 'What were you thinking?'

'Don't ask.'

'Then I know.'

'You have noticed?'

'Of course I have noticed. Everyone has. You don't expect such things to be secret?'

'Nothing has happened.'

'I don't believe you.'

'It is foolish.'

'Once you start to love,' said Shirin, 'it is hard to want to stop.'

'I have loved once. Isn't that enough? Was that not my fate?'

'No. And perhaps it is time to leave mourning behind.'

'I do not want to betray the memory.'

'Dujan would have married again.'

'I am not talking about marriage.'

'But you are talking about love.'

'Yes, I am,' said Aisha simply. 'I would like to love again. To be saved.'

'He will be leaving soon,' said Shirin. 'Perhaps he will never return. Why not love him now?'

'Because I do not want to hurt him. And I do not want to lose him, to suffer loss again.'

'But you are not happy.'

'Do you think I am mad?'

'No, I think you are fortunate.'

'I do not feel fortunate.'

'You are.' Shirin finished bandaging the hand.

Aisha met her sister's eye. 'Do you think I should continue to see him, even if I know he must leave?'

'He may return. Has he said so?'

'He has.'

187

'And you believe him?'

'Yes,' said Aisha, 'I do.'

She considered Paolo once more: his strange serious-ness. I love this man, she thought.

ೞ

When Aisha saw Paolo again she hardly knew what to say. It was the first time he had seen her so nervous, and he was anxious about her hand. Yet when he tried to comfort her, he found her quite resistant.

'If you are so worried then you could stay now, without leaving, and look after me,' she challenged.

'You know that I have a duty.'

'And I know that you could send the men on with the stone without you.'

'I must go. I made my promise. As I have promised to you. Then, I hope you can see what it means.'

'That is easy to say now.'

'Then come with me.'

'You know that I cannot.'

'Then wait.'

Aisha suddenly felt short of breath. Why were they speaking like this? 'Poets tell us that love is always increasing or decreasing and it never stays the same. One always loves more than the other: the lover and the loved.'

'Then our task is to make it constant, unchanging . . .' said Paolo.

'Until death.'

'That is what the priests tell us.'

'And do you hope for another life, beyond the stars?' she asked.

'I would rather return here and find you again, loving in this world and this world only, without hope of another.'

'Think what such a love might mean.' Aisha looked out to the dying fires. 'Think of your life.'

'Our life,' he interrupted.

'Your life. Your future. You should not love me. I must set you free from me. It is not right.'

'And if I say that it is?' he asked.

'It is not.'

Paolo turned to face her. 'You are worried about Jamal.'

'No. I am worried about you.'

'I cannot be his father.'

'No.'

'But I can try to be his brother. And I can say that I will always love you.' Paolo paused. 'I know this.'

He thought that Aisha had stopped listening, that she did not want to hear these words, but then she cried out: 'But will you love me? Do you love me? I cannot lose again. My heart cannot be made soft only to break once more.'

'It is the only thing in life of which I am sure.'

Aisha stopped, leaned forward, and they kissed once more. Perhaps this was what death was like, Paolo wondered, this surrender.

Then Aisha pulled away. At first Paolo thought she

might cry, shuddering against him, but, instead, she stepped back and looked into his eyes.

'Love me,' she said.

ಗಿಲ

The next morning Salek looked up at the hard blue sky. 'From now on it will freeze every night. Tomorrow we must leave,' he told Jacopo. 'We have stayed too long.'

'I must inform the woman,' said Jacopo. 'Come with me.'

'And who will tell the boy? Perhaps he has plans to stay,' Salek replied.

'I will tell him,' said Jacopo. 'He must learn again what it is to say farewell.'

They could see the women gathering the last of the mulberries in the distance. Salek was right, thought Jacopo; they had stayed too long. Now it was time. Any more lapis would be hard to carry.

'You are not happy here?' asked Aisha.

'We have been made welcome. And you have shown true friendship. But we have trade in Cathay. Salek has said that we must leave before the winter or we will be stranded.'

'Would that be so bad?'

'We would be a burden,' said Salek. 'We would diminish your food.'

'And you will take the stone?'

'With gratitude.'

She felt the fear and sickness of loss. The dread

returned: the withdrawal of love, the end of happiness. How could she have been so foolish, committing herself so far even when she knew that it must finish? 'Paolo will be sad.'

'We have no choice.'

'Then tonight,' said Aisha brightly, but without quite knowing what she was saying, 'we must feast.'

ॐ

The evening was brilliant and clear, and although the sun was bright on the snow, it was too cold to provide warmth. Two of the women began to make kumis, beating mare's milk in great leather bags suspended from frames until the whey separated from the curds. Others prepared boal from honey. Paolo knew their names – Zuleika and Amaba, Rabia and Shirin, Leila and Durkhani. Another group of women were roasting a sheep over a full fire, making pilau and kabābs.

A low horn sounded to announce the beginning of the feast. Aisha dipped her fingers in the bowl of kumis and smeared the mouths of their household gods with drink. Then she cut away sections of meat from the sheep on the spit and laid them before each of the idols.

'Protect us, gods of our fathers, and gods of our sons who have been and shall be. We honour you as you honour us.'

As she bowed before them Jacopo became alarmed. 'I cannot take part in this.'

'Leave them,' said Salek. 'They will not trouble you.'

The women gave each of the men a bowl of rice wine,

sesame paste, chilli, and soy. They were to take the meat, finish its cooking in the collective broth, and then dip it in their sauce.

Salek picked up his meat with a wooden spoon. *'Strength to your arm, God be praised, long life to you, may you not be tired.'*

Jacopo ignored the meat. 'It will trouble my heart. What I would give for some good Jewish food: latkes, kugel, or kreplach. It is nearly Chanukah. And what I would give for some rugelach,' he mused. 'Even chicken. If they just had chicken, I would be happy.'

'Stop complaining,' whispered Paolo.

'Who's complaining?' said Jacopo. He took the bread and the pilau, and drank from the kumis. 'Let a man dream.'

The women sat in a circle, banging drums, chanting defiant songs of love and war. Salek began to smoke a pipe. Jacopo lay on his back and looked up at the stars.

Warmed by the fire, filled by meat, and enlivened by the kumis, a quiet satisfaction spread through the community. For one night they did not need to think of their troubled past or uncertain future. Some of the women began to dance.

Aisha gestured that Paolo should sit on the ground beside her. 'Look at the sky,' she said. 'Watch it darken. It can change almost as quickly as a life.'

She put her arm around him, and pulled him towards her for warmth. 'Look now: the darkest blue before the black.'

Together they watched the clouds fold into the darkness, each detail fading as the stars rose. They were as numberless as the dead.

Still looking up into the sky, Aisha said simply: 'And so you are going?'

'You know that I have to.'

'No. You do not have to. You want to. But let us not argue.'

Paolo took her hand. Without thinking he began to stroke it, following the line of her fingers. 'As I was cutting the stone in the cave today I found insects living inside it, hidden away. They were unaware of the stone, they did not fear it, and so moved on. Plants grow there: in the stone and out of the darkness. That is like love. The stone may be as powerful as fate, impossibly so, and yet it can be broken. It needs to be broken; and life emerges, stronger than the stone from which it came.'

They kissed, his head tilting away from her eye, so that he could no longer see her clearly. He closed his eyes and felt his body fall away, abandoning all thoughts of his past or his future, wanting only this moment.

Aisha stopped as if to check herself, curious, and frightened. Paolo opened his eyes, and she was staring directly into them. He brought up his hand to shield the brightness, looking only at her, wanting no other light. Now he could see clearly, more sharply than he had ever seen anything before.

'Come with me,' said Aisha, taking him towards her tent. 'Come with me now.'

They could speak about anything; they could dream and talk and be as vulnerable and as afraid as they had always been but had never been able to say. They held each other and knew that this passing moment between sleep and waking, this blur between dream and reality could defy time. Aisha pulled off her dress, raising it above her head, and Paolo was astonished by her naked-ness. He took off his clothes, amazed by the softness of flesh against flesh, life against life. Before, he had only been half himself. Now he was complete. His life had meaning. Nothing would ever matter as much as this again.

❧

The next morning he awoke with a start. Someone was shaking him, pulling him away from all that he had found.

'Come, we are ready.' It was Salek. 'Leave her. Get dressed.'

'I cannot,' said Paolo.

'You must. Everything is packed. We have done all this for you.' Salek pulled Paolo out of the bed, picked up his clothes, and threw them at him.

Aisha stirred and sat up, pulling the coverings against her.

'We must leave,' said Salek. 'You know this.'

'Then let me say farewell.'

Now Jamal pushed past Salek. He had come to find his mother. He stopped as soon as he saw Paolo dressing.

'Why are you going?' he asked. It was the first time he had spoken to him.

'I have to.'

'Quickly,' said Salek. 'We are already late.'

'For what?' asked Paolo.

'There may be a storm. Come now.'

Jamal pulled at Paolo's arm. 'Stay,' he said.

'He cannot,' said Salek, and Paolo knew that it was true.

'I will come back.' Paolo gathered up his bag and ruffled Jamal's hair. He turned to Aisha. 'You know that. I have promised.'

'Here,' she said, 'take this.' She picked up a coat made from animal skin.

Paolo leaned forward and kissed her once more.

Salek interrupted. 'No time. Come.'

Aisha gripped Paolo's arms. 'Think of us.'

'I will think of nothing else.'

Jacopo was waiting outside. Paolo tried to focus but could only see low black clouds coming towards him. The cold air was at them, sharp and unremitting. The snow on the ground lifted and swirled in the wind, the sharpness of its grit spitting in their faces.

'Help us,' shouted Jacopo. 'Hold on to the animals.'

Paolo took the reins Jacopo gave him and felt the mules pull away from him, desperate for shelter or escape. Ahead he could see Salek shouting through the rain: 'Ride.'

They forced their way through the storm, challenging its power. The rain streaked across Jacopo's face and the indigo dye of his beard coloured the drops of water running down his neck.

'We must go on,' called Salek. 'Move. It will only get worse.'

The track ahead had been transformed into a thick mud, which clung to the mules' hooves. They struggled forward, and the rain lessened enough for them to realise the extent of the storm, to feel the cold and wet that now enveloped them.

'I told you we should have left earlier,' shouted Salek.

Paolo had never felt so alone.

At last they found shelter in a narrow lee. Salek unsaddled his mule and began to erect a tent but it was so wet it had to be wrung dry. Nothing had escaped the storm.

'We must make fire. Dry these. Tonight it might freeze and everything will be as ice – our tent, our clothes, our food. You must find wood. I will light what we have. Go.'

Paolo pulled a branch from a tree, ripping it away so strongly that a section of bark cut into his hand. He looked at the blood and remembered the way Aisha had caressed his face. He felt the ache of tenderness gone from his life and tried to think of every possible way in which he could see her again.

Soon it would be night. The air bit into their bones. They lit the damp fire and sat round it, bleak in the cold, without speaking. Then they ate thin herb soup with nan bread.

Paolo felt as if his body were no longer his own. The world had dulled; even its beauty. The brilliance of the sky, the vast stretch of rock, the open horizon before him meant nothing. It no longer mattered what he ate or where he travelled. He drifted without energy or purpose, as if the vital spark that ignited and drove his life had been removed. Every action he performed – standing, walking, or moving in any way – required an energy that he was no longer sure he possessed.

He lay down, knowing that the last time he had done so had been with Aisha. Perhaps this was now his task – to remember her, willing all other memories to disappear in order to be replaced by the rush of love. He would think of Aisha's eyes half closing as she kissed him, the way her breathing changed, the moistness on the upper rim of her lips. He dreamed of her caress in the half-waking, half-sleeping darkness; and the knowledge that it was all he wanted.

He tried to remember the pores of her skin against his flesh, the quickening pulse in her wrist, and the rise and fall of her breathing: all beauty contained in that moment.

For the next few days, weeks, or months, as long as they travelled, he would try to live in memory alone.

TUN-HUANG

Now they travelled east, through narrow passes and under heavy peaks, towards Cathay, sheltering in hollows and on raised ledges, making camp wherever they could. The snow often wiped away all tracks of the previous day and when fog descended it was almost impossible for the men to find their bearings. Paolo set up signs each night, pointing in the direction they wished to travel the next morning, hammering down the tents, making their possessions secure.

The three companions stopped whenever there was water, and the rivers began to fill with the winter rains. They set out traps for animals and survived on raisins and dried mulberries, the bread they made and the water they carried. When the men were hungry they dreamed of meat – lamb, chicken, rabbit, marmot, and gazelle. Salek told them how merchants from his village would slaughter a sheep, skin it, cut it into pieces, and throw it down the sides of the mountain into the valleys, hoping that precious stones would adhere to the stickiness of fresh, bloody meat.

As they approached Cathay the vegetation became richer and they found themselves in a grove of bamboo trees, stretching out into the distance. At last there was lushness, a swathe of green, the possibility of spring. The bamboo bent low under the weight of the snow, snapping as suddenly as a broken bone. The men cut the first of the new shoots and heated them with boiled rice, their purple nodules like old brocade, the white skin coloured like pearls. When it was necessary to cross a river they made a raft from the bamboo, lashing each rod with hemp.

When they finally arrived they discovered that the streets of Tun-huang were filled with traders, water-sellers, dancers, acrobats, musicians, and singing girls. Noodle makers offered breakfast delicacies of mutton and goose, steamed pancakes and fragrant rice. The women of the city hung branches of willow over their doorways and prepared marrow soup, swallows' nests smoked with slices of duck, and beef with ginger, star anise, and rock sugar.

Salek spoke to a man selling firecrackers made from sticks of bamboo packed with gunpowder. He told them that they had arrived in time for his play of explosions, and that in the evening he would light the sky, challenging the heavens with fire.

Paolo had never seen Jacopo so at ease in his surroundings. Before them stood the Jade Gate decorated with carved lions and gleaming with a translucent green light. Beyond he could see piles of the jewel on the traders' tables: snow white, emerald green, lavender blue. Men worked with cutting tools, treadle wheels, whetstones, and polishing paste to shape the precious objects that lay before them: triple hoops, rings, amulets, pendants, and necklaces; hairpins decorated with pearl-eyed dragons breathing ruby flames; jadeite drops and pearls the size of canary eggs. Everything that might celebrate life, decorate existence, or protect the wearer against evil lay before them. Paolo could see mountains in stone, forests in agate, rivers in marble, and faces in jasper. The jade was so pure that the traders believed it could preserve flesh from decay, raise the dead, strike down the faithless, and protect a spirit on its journey into the afterlife.

Jacopo began to test a piece of rough stone, longing to know what might happen when the rock revealed its secrets. 'When the skin of jade is one inch thick, even the immortals cannot guess what lies within.'

'How long will we stay?' Paolo asked.

'You must help me. Hidden here are jewels of lesser worth, fakes, and forgeries. I must hold each stone, weigh it, see it, and even try to mark it. And then, when I know, when I have truly looked, we can trade and return.'

A loud gong interrupted the conversation. The jade merchants packed up their stalls, firecrackers shot up into the sky, and the town was transformed into a festival of light and heat, food and noise. Wheels of coloured fire spun in circles in the distance. Rockets shot upwards.

Paolo could see the fireworks reflected on the lake, as water and horizon became one. Clouds of smoke burst open with fountains of colour, spraying, spurting, and cracking into life. He had never heard such noise, ripping into and against the wind, challenging destiny and darkness.

'*Huo yao tsa hsi,*' said a man, laughing and pointing, trying to explain what was happening. He scurried amidst the fireworks, crouching down, lighting rockets. He looked out into the distance and up into the sky, pleased with his work. He asked the crowds to keep away, but Salek urged Paolo to look more closely at the man as he sent flames into the air. The fireworks were reflected in circles of quartz in front of his eyes, tied with a leather strap around the back of his head.

Paolo edged closer. The man was wearing spectacles, but they were different from any that he had seen before, and they seemed to allow a clear view of the night sky. He could see into the distance.

The next day Paolo insisted that Salek ask for the fire-work maker's workshop. If the man could help him then perhaps he would be able to find true perspective at last. It was so long since he had tried such lenses in Venice that he had almost forgotten how frustrating the experience had been. But now he was filled with hope. Clarity of vision could, at last, be a liberation from the frustration of an out-of-focus world, as if surfacing from underwater into the sharp clarity of day.

They joined the early-morning crowds travelling out to

the fields on the edge of the city and stopped at a separate compound, far away from any other building, made of stone and fired clay. The governor had decreed that firework makers were even more dangerous than bakers or potters and must be kept well apart from other businesses. He knew how easily a conflagration could take hold.

Paolo and Salek passed through a spirit gate and entered a small courtyard filled with piles of bamboo and small wooden barrels stacked neatly on raised platforms. Through a half-open doorway they could see the silhouette of a man asleep in a low bed behind a screen of wood and rice paper.

'He is probably drunk,' said Salek. 'Let us fetch him water.'

'Why can't we wait?'

'He has been celebrating all night. But if we give him something to drink then he will thank us.'

They collected water from the courtyard, carrying it back in a wooden bucket, and then sat beside the firework maker. Salek tried to shake him gently awake, but the man only grunted and turned over.

Paolo saw the spectacles lying on a low table. Unlike the familiar pebble lenses, these were their opposite, cut quartz, with polished faces, thin in the middle and thick at the edges. He reached over and picked them up, feeling their weight in his hand, examining the leather and bone bridge that supported the two lenses. Then he held them up to his eyes. Objects in the room became dazzlingly sharp. Clearer shapes and intricate textures came into focus in an expanded vision for the first time. Lengths of bamboo leaning against the wall; iron tools lying on benches; powders and scales, striker lights, flints, and charcoal; all these objects now made him part of a composition that helped Paolo place himself more solidly in the world.

Salek shook the sleeping man again. He stirred and reached out for the glasses by the bed, patting the surface of the table, trying to find where he had left them.

The lenses were still in Paolo's hands.

The man sat up, his eyes still closed, and groped for the spectacles again. He could see nothing without them.

'Here,' said Paolo.

The firework maker looked confused. Perhaps he was still dreaming. He put on his glasses and stared at his visitors with surprise, inquiring what they were doing in his workshop at this time of the morning. Then he dipped a beaker into the bucket of water and drank it in one draught. He filled it again, dipped his fingers, and rubbed his eyes between the lids and the lenses, washing himself awake.

'You would come to know my secrets?'

'We would.'

'They are not to be shared. I can sell you my goods, but the recipes are sacred from the ancients.'

'It is not flame that we seek,' said Salek.

'Then why are you here?'

'I want to know where I can obtain the lenses that you use, the quartz against your eyes,' said Paolo.

The firework maker smiled, pointing to his spectacles.
'I made them.'

'You appear to see far off, into the distance. I watched you. You saw both the sky and the fireworks clearly.'

'Yes, I see as well as anyone with these.'

'Can you show me how you make them?'

The firework maker looked at Paolo as if assessing whether he was worthy of his secrets. 'What would you give for such sight?'

'Almost all that I have.'

'Almost?'

'Stone. Jewels. Goods. Money.'

'But if I make them for you, to see the world differently, perhaps you will not like it.'

'I want to see it clearly.'

'And you are sure you can accept what might happen if you do?'

'I cannot imagine it, but I am prepared to accept the risk and pay the price you think fit.'

'Then come,' said the man suddenly.

In the workshop a group of men gathered round low benches making candles and rockets, concocting great arrows of flame that could be shot into the sky with a crossbow, poisonous smoke balls, flame-throwers, incendiary whip arrows, fire pots, underwater bombs, and paper bags filled with quicklime and sulphur that would explode on contact with water. The firework maker showed Paolo rip-rack crackers and fire lances, fiery oil in bowls, iron-headed military rockets, and even an explosive basket of eggs. He told them how he could colour the sky with fire and flame, making blue smoke from woad, purple flames with indigo, violet from cinnabar, and yellow from saffron and sulphur.

Salek stayed back, watching the workers cut lengths of bamboo, boring holes into the side, strengthening the base with cladding and then packing each section with explosives.

The firework maker took Paolo past a yellow curtain into a room that was filled with light: the opposite of everything they had just encountered. This second workshop glowed with honeyed warmth, and on each table lay lentil-shaped pebbles of beryl and quartz, cut and polished in various sizes and shapes, each scattering the light around the room in cascades of mirrored reflection.

'This is where I help people to see,' said the firework maker, bowing. 'I am Chen.'

'Paolo.'

Chen asked his visitor to sit on a mat in front of an open window. Then he prepared a series of lenses of different thicknesses on a small tray. He placed these lenses in front of Paolo's eyes, asking his patient to describe the distortions he noticed in the window and in the distant horizon. At one extreme it was like viewing the world through the top of a perfume bottle. Through trial and error, Chen slowly began to eliminate those lenses that would not help Paolo's vision; first the left eye, then the right, each needing separate attention to obtain the sharpest sight. At times, Paolo thought that he was looking through a tunnel, and the goods in the workshop became strangely disorientating, threatening, as if in a dream; his head hurt with the confusion as he tried to re-orientate himself. Some lenses made him struggle to find any focus. The concentration needed made his brain swim.

Chen loomed large before him as he inspected every part of Paolo's eyes, carefully examining the pupils by pulling the flesh down, asking him to look up to the heavens, down to the earth, and across to each edge of the world. Paolo had never looked into a man's eyes so clearly. They were the colour of hazel.

Chen held a candle up against Paolo's eyes, asking him to follow it as he moved it from left to right. His breath smelled of rice wine, and he breathed heavily, as if already exhausted by the process.

'Close your left eye.' He held up an almond-shaped piece of quartz. 'Now look through this.'

'It is misty. Dark.'

'Can you see the distance more clearly, even through this stone?'

'No.'

'If the lens has not been completely ground then the view is distorted. Try this.'

'Better.'

'And the other eye?'

'No. Another.'

Chen held a piece of beryl to the left eye. 'I need to

check the shape of the stone and the way it curves. Can you see more clearly with these?'

'I'm not sure. I do not know if my sight will ever improve as yours has done.'

'You see the clear stone that is used to magnify things close. Look at it. Turn it over in your hand. Hold it up between your eye and my eye.'

Paolo experimented once again with distance, seeing how Chen's eyes grew and diminished.

'It is convex. It curves outwards. Like your eyes. They see close objects too clearly, while the distance is dim. The mountains are large, perhaps grander than they are in life, but they are also faint. Everything is far away. That perhaps is why your travels have been so long. You want to arrive on the summit of the mountain but you are always reaching for the unreachable, as if you were running towards a rainbow before it fades. It is always a blur. You live in a landscape where nothing can be seen in context. As soon as you realise where you are, you are too close to see what such a place might mean.'

'And the world bends . . .'

'The world curves around you because your eyes themselves have too much curvature. Now we must make a lens that compensates for this distortion.'

'But when I put quartz in front of my eyes everything is as milk.'

'We must polish this quartz and make a lens that is doubly concave, thicker at the edges than in the middle.

But we must take care not to crack or split the delicate centre which bends the light in your favour.'

He took two rough quartz pebbles. Then he began to grind away at each pebble in a circular motion, hollowing the centre, smoothing the surface into a curvature to match the grinding stone. He kept turning the lenses over, checking each side, polishing them into shape with a mixture of powder and emery, holding the quartz up to the light between each stage, verifying the translucency, proceeding silently with utter concentration lest the quartz cracked or shattered.

'Come outside so that we can see into the distance more clearly.'

The air was crisp; the sky cobalt blue. Chen held a lens up to the right eye, and the distant mountain immediately sharpened into focus. Paolo thought that he could see a group of women dyeing cloth by the river; but, close to, objects were blurred, as if his sight had been reversed.

'Wait. I need to adjust the curvature of the right lens, and polish the front of the left.'

Paolo felt as if his new-found sight had been snatched away from him. 'How long will this take?'

'Not long.'

Chen went back inside and re-worked the lens surfaces. He ground them down, adjusting their curvature, which he then checked against a series of curved wooden templates on his workbench.

'Why is it so hard?' asked Paolo.

'Convex shapes are everywhere in nature, like the drop

of water on a leaf, a teardrop, or weather-worn pebbles shaped by wind, water, and rain. They are solid, strong, and natural. Here we are working against nature. This is unstable, thin in the middle, easily broken. The rock crystal can shatter. We must hope for luck that we find the right curve for you, a lens that bends the light to correct your sight.'

He continued to polish each lens in circling movements, and at last the crystal began to emerge, glittering with reflected light.

Chen held each lens and checked its clarity. Then Paolo took both carefully between his fingers and raised them to his eyes. The previous world lurched into focus. He could see into Chen's eye, watching him, smiling hopefully.

'Yes, these.'

'Let me finish them.'

Chen took a piece of iron with a fine point and bored holes into each side of the almond-shaped lenses. Then he threaded a piece of leather in a metal clasp through the two inner holes to form a supporting bridge. He reached for a pair of calipers and measured the circumference of Paolo's head before cutting a second piece of leather to length, finally tying the glasses in a knot at the back.

Paolo began to test and adjust the lenses in front of his eyes, trying to find the most comfortable place for them to sit, seeing the whorls of his fingers up close against him. He blinked and began to readjust his vision, looking out into the distance, as if he lived in two different worlds: one close to, the other far off.

They walked into the streets and Paolo could see lanterns receding far ahead, green, red, and white, hanging in the doorways of every shop front. They swayed gently in the breeze against embroidered beads or jade curtains, but now, instead of witnessing the scene through frosted glass, he saw each lantern whole, clearly defined, one from another. There were lanterns that turned under a trickle of water; others were shaped as boats and dragons, with horses and horsemen, or as gods and goddesses decorated in gold and silver, pearls and jade.

He looked back at Chen, who now appeared too close, too large, before him, the lines on his forehead as distinct as if they were inches rather than feet apart. He took the glasses away from his eyes, and then raised them once more, testing the sudden shock of sight.

For the first time Paolo could see the thickness of clouds, their depth, detail, and texture. He felt a rush of vision, and almost stumbled at the new world around him. His gaze became so highly focused that everything he saw had acquired a concentrated clarity.

He tried to walk, but felt disorientated, as if he had just disembarked from a ship in a foreign country. Objects appeared to hurtle towards him. They came so close and so quickly that his head began to ache, pained by the clarity of the world. Scribes and acrobats, fortune-tellers, astrologers, palm-readers, prophets, and seers crowded past. They walked more quickly, came into vision more swiftly, and departed too soon. The world had suddenly become fast.

Was this how Aisha saw?

He walked away, out through the tanneries, and saw the rich saffron, scarlet, mint, and antimony dyes of the women, their arms coloured, bright cloths curtaining their homes to shade against sun and brightness. A bare-chested, muscular man with stained arms pulled stretches of indigo-dyed cotton out of a vat that had been hollowed from the earth. He rinsed it clear so that the water turned a dark and violent blue. The stain followed the veins of his arms. Paolo had never noticed the blood beneath another man's skin before.

He saw the women reeling silk, making looms, and rearing worms. He noticed, for the first time, the threads hanging from the mouths of the silkworm caterpillars, the white circles near the breast and head, the three-fold spur in their tails.

Now he could read the letters on the votive strips that hung from the trees above a potter glazing a set of bowls. He stood, waited, and watched the transformation as the cobalt glaze became a rich deep blue. He saw the pots cooling in sand, and looked through the peephole into the orange glow of the kiln as the potter waited for the glaze to become as golden as sunlight on snow.

The smoke and heat of the potteries reached up into his eyes, which now began to smart. A pedlar offered him hot water and Paolo took off his glasses. He scooped the water from the bowl and felt the warmth and the wetness cleanse and heal. He reached for a cloth and patted his eyes dry. When he opened them again, the water still clung to his eyelids and he felt his vision swim. He blinked against the light. And then, when he could see again without his spectacles, he saw that the earth had returned to its former mist.

All this time he had looked with soft eyes.

He put on the spectacles once more. His head ached with the excitement of the new possibilities before him. At the same time the world became threatening, as objects loomed into view, good and evil, without any differentiation, sharply defined before him, like a clear and sudden view of death.

And the town was louder now. The cries of children, the barking of dogs, and the shouting in the market came from every direction: ahead, behind, from the sides, above, and below. The sounds met each other in Paolo, travelled through him, and bounced back off the walls to hit him again with their reverberation, echo upon echo, so that he was no longer sure which way he was walking. The noise had become cacophonous. He had to get back to the firework maker, talk to him, and ask him to explain. Was the world meant to be so clear and so sharp; or did the lenses contain some dark magic within them?

'What do you think?' asked Chen.

'It is too much,' replied Paolo. 'I feel like a blind man who has been granted sight . . .'

'If they are too strong . . .'

'Let me walk a while,' replied Paolo. 'Let me try to get used to them . . .'

'You will need time . . .'

'I am two people now: one who can see and one who cannot.'

'Then you must decide which man you wish to be,' said Chen. 'Clear vision is painful as well as enlightening. The further we see into the distance, the more we understand its limitations.'

ॐ

Salek and Jacopo were amused by Paolo's new-found sight and celebrated by buying three kites which they flew from a hill on the edge of the town.

Paolo watched the paper stream across the sky, a great wave of red against blue, and felt hope at last. He longed to go home and show his parents that he could see. He wanted to tell Simone, not only to give him the stone with which he could paint eternal life, but also to explain what it meant. For he knew now, with each vista that opened up before him, with every sense of distance, what it might be like to paint space, to imagine infinity.

'At least we won't lose any more animals,' said Salek. 'You can see when they are camels and when they are rocks.'

'I can see everything. Even when you are teasing me. Before I had to guess when you were being serious and when you were not. Now I can read your face.'

'We never tease you. We are your friends,' said Jacopo.

'I am not so sure of that.'

'Sometimes,' said Salek, 'I think you are ungrateful. We have shown you the world. Now you can see it clear.'

'I do not know that I always want to do that. It is so sharp, so lustrous. Sometimes I want to close my eyes and let the brightness pass.'

'There will be time enough to close your eyes,' said Jacopo.

'One day' – Paolo smiled – 'just for one day on this journey, it would be good not to be reminded of death. You have taught me, and taught me well. I have learned my lesson, and it does not need to be repeated. And so perhaps you could refrain from referring to the fact of our mortality each time we discuss our lives. Is that too much to ask? Do you think you could do this? Just for one day?'

'I do not think so,' said Salek.

'Impossible,' agreed Jacopo.

ဢ

Over the next few days, Paolo's earliest doubts and uncertainties began to take hold. Despite the sharpness and the brightness he also saw flaw and decay in everything around him. He could see how furrowed a brow could be and how swiftly a man aged. He saw disease, blisters, wounds, and unhappiness. He noticed, for the first time, that the bundles of rags lying in the road, and abandoned at regular intervals, contained people. He could see them clearly, arms outstretched, their faces wrought with pain. Perhaps God had given him short sight to protect him from such clarity; and the lenses were, after all, an aberration, a disavowal of the divine plan for his life. Paolo felt like a man who had been given all the riches of the world and only longed once more for his poverty.

He talked to Chen's customers. People came who thought that they would never see again: a man who wanted to watch his son fly a kite in the sky before he died; an astronomer who wanted to help his brother to see what he saw, mapping the heavens, understanding the divinity of creation. There was a nobleman who wanted spectacles for his horse, and a lady who was convinced that such a device might help her cat kill more mice. Another man came because he wanted to spy on the courtesans of the city, asking Chen if he could make a lens that might let him see through their clothes without payment; while a wife brought her husband a pair of spectacles to make him aware of the flaws of women he had wanted to seduce.

One man came and complained that he saw too clearly. He asked for spectacles to cloud his vision so that he could not see long distances so sharply. He wanted to live in a narrower, shorter world: to live, as Paolo had done, with softer eyes.

Chen told Paolo that he should spend a day and a night looking at the sky to soothe his eyes and calm his thoughts. If he wanted to see beauty he should always look upwards.

'Imagine the sky is the eyeball of our creator,' said Chen, 'curved in its socket, looking down upon us.'

Paolo should study the clouds, and trace the colour of the heavens as they changed from dawn to day and from dusk into the night, taking his thoughts away from the frailty and vanity of mankind. To look up at the sky was to know one's place in the universe: the light of the setting sun over the mountains was the halo of Buddha.

Paolo watched the stars and the colour of the night sky through all its clouds and clarity and wanted to tell Aisha that now he saw as she did. He saw the moon as a crescent illuminated against a darker sphere. Before, it had always been a patch of white. Now he could see its dark planes and far craters.

When he returned he told Chen how the world served only to remind him of the suffering it contained, the love he had lost, and the futility of his own existence.

'I am sorry to hear you say this.'

'I am sorry to feel it. What can I do?'

'If the sky does not bring you comfort then you must go to see my father.'

'He will help me?'

'He is a holy man. He does not always speak. But he knows of the sorrows of the world. That is why he has withdrawn from it.'

'But does he see the world clearly? With all its faults and yet know what it is to live within it? Does he believe there is a purpose, even if this life is all there is?'

'It is his only concern, his daily hope,' replied Chen.

ಬಬ

It was the eighth day of the fourth moon. Approached through a grove of elms and poplars, the caves of the Ch'ien-fo-tung lay to the southeast on a steep bare slope of the Altyn Tagh range of mountains. Inscribed silken banners hung from the cliffs, stretching hundreds of feet down to the ground. A honeycomb of rock temples paid tribute to the dream of Lo-tsun, a monk who once had a vision of a thousand Buddhas in a cloud of glory.

The head lama was a small man who combined religious certainty with an air of distrust, as if he were far more confident of the next life than he was of this. He asked if Paolo had come to trade or to seek wisdom. If the former, then he required candles, lamp oil, small metal cups, and bowls; if the latter, then his journey need go no further.

The caves stretched back into the darkness, each lit by a series of small flames. Here people prepared to scale the ladder, climb the tree, cross the perilous bridge, ford the river or ascend the mountain to the blaze of heaven. Some of the monks were making images: first in straw, and then covering them with clay before firing, glazing, and firing again. Others contemplated the paintings on the dark walls: Avalokitesvara with eleven heads and a thousand arms, cock-headed demons on pothi leaves, the lotus pond of paradise, or scenes from the life of the Buddha. Pilgrims lit silver lamps at shrines whose light pierced the darkness of the sky. Travellers intoned from sacred texts, made offerings, and burned incense, either praying for protection as they embarked on the start of their journey over the silk route, or thanking the gods for their safe return.

Chen's father was meditating.

He was a tall man with a shaved head and an expression that was more determined than serene. He wore a yellow robe, and sat perfectly still, his twisted feet bent back in the lotus position. His strength and vigour suggested that he must once have been a warrior.

Chen and Paolo sat and watched.

An hour passed.

Paolo looked at every head and every arm of the painting of Avalokitesvara on the wall of the cave; he tried to analyse what made each detail different but could only surmise that they all seemed the same.

Another hour passed.

He wondered what it would be like to walk around with eleven heads. Was one head in charge of the other ten, or were they all equal? Were there eleven brains, each with different roles and responsibilities? And what must it be like to carry a thousand arms with you as you walked? There must be five hundred on each side of the body. Paolo thought that reproduction would also be a problem but he supposed that the gods were beyond such desires. Still, he thought, it would involve a great deal of grappling if it ever happened, never mind the eleven heads.

Paolo listened to the monk's breathing. It was shallow, almost imperceptible, with a long intake and a slow release. The three men sat in silence. When Paolo could bear it no longer he asked Chen if anything else might happen.

'Those who speak know nothing; those who know are silent.'

Finally the father opened his eyes, although he kept staring ahead.

Paolo realised that this was the only event of any interest that had happened in the previous four hours.

'This is Paolo,' Chen said at last.

The monk turned, nodded, and remained silent. Perhaps he was still in a trance.

'I am troubled,' Paolo said quietly. 'Now I have spectacles I see the world too clearly.'

Chen's father answered at last. 'And what do you see?'

Paolo paused and wondered what he did see. The central line of wrinkles on the monk's forehead. His small brown eyes. The saffron of his gown. The flower floating in the bowl of water in front of him. He looked away, out to a bamboo grove in the distance.

'I see the leaf of every tree.'

The monk nodded, as if he understood; but how could he know what it was like? How could he live as Paolo lived?

'Then take time to study.'

'Every leaf?'

'Each leaf. Or one leaf. From spring through to summer. Its rise and its sap, the greening and the fall. In one year you will understand all years.'

He had already spent one night looking at the sky darken and then lighten again. 'You want me to spend a year looking at a leaf?'

'It is not me who should want such a thing. I have no wants and no wishes. It is you who must want it: as the leaf needs to grow and then fall, so must you.'

'Such a long time.'

'One of our ancestors, Bodhidharma, spent nine years in meditation facing a wall. Great things are disclosed through the small. You will be glad of the leaf.'

'And if I cannot do this?'

'Come to me again when you can.'

ಬಬ

For the next few days Paolo tried to ignore the monk's advice but found that the idea would not leave his head. He must try such an experiment, however absurd. Perhaps he would learn more from standing still than he ever had from travelling.

His only mistake was to tell Salek and Jacopo.

'I do not understand,' said Jacopo. 'First you want to stay with that woman. Now you want to live with a leaf.'

'How will you ever return home?' asked Salek.

'I will come whenever you are ready,' Paolo replied.

'Then we look forward to hearing of your adventures.' Jacopo smiled. 'Perhaps the leaf would like to join us on our return? I anticipate much philosophical conversation both with the leaf, and, indeed, upon it.'

Paolo walked out to find a cherry tree at the end of a

long avenue on the edge of the town. The ground was damp with dew. He attempted the lotus position, just as the monk had sat, but could not manoeuvre his legs in the correct manner. Never had his body seemed so unyielding, as if his limbs were too long. In fact he could not find a single position in which he could relax and concentrate. He tried to lie on his side, but the ground felt even harder. There was a chill in the air, and he found that he could think of nothing but the damp earth beneath him.

'Om,' he said, half-heartedly.

Nothing happened.

'Om, Om, Om, Om.'

He wondered if he should abandon this activity, but to return now, so soon, would admit failure, and he could not face scorn from Jacopo or laughter from Salek.

An hour passed before he decided to lie down on his back and look up at the tree, watching the light filter through the leaves.

He was surprised by the difference between the leaves. Upon which one should he concentrate? Perhaps this was the message of the monk: to find his own life in the midst of so many.

He looked at a branch already gnarled with age.

A pale-green leaf, lighter than jade, nestled under a piece of blossom.

He wondered if he could not meditate because he was frightened of what he might find. Perhaps that is why he had never stopped for long enough to think further on what his life had meant and what it might become.

There was a light breeze and the tree began to sway. A flock of cranes flew low against the horizon.

Paolo watched the leaf cling to the tree. Would it weaken in the wind or darken in the sun? Would it hold the rain? How would it nourish itself?

He wanted to look at the trunk of the tree and sense the sap rising, the tree nourishing itself from the earth, but did not want to take his eyes away from the leaf. He wondered if he should be hungry or thirsty, and then, as he gazed at the leaf, he began to lose the sense of his own body, its dampness and its discomfort.

'I could lie here for ever,' he thought.

He began to concentrate on his own breathing. He tried to slow down his heartbeat, and to become aware only of his breath, keeping the leaf alive. Every exhalation, steady and regular, reached out towards the leaf.

His breath. And the leaf.

He now lived in the moment alone. He was outside both memory and time. If the dreams came again, then they came. And if death came, then it came.

Now he wanted to look at the leaf in a different way, examining the curve of its side, its undulation, and its resolution, the fineness of its point.

He stood up and reached for the branch, pulling it down towards him so that he could study it more closely.

The branch bent, cracking quietly as Paolo examined the dark-green sheen on the surface. Should he touch it, feeling its fragility in his hands? Or should he test its strength? How sharply would he have to pull to sever the leaf from the tree? How much before its time would the leaf then die?

Or, if he let nature take its course, how long would he have to wait for the leaf to fall of its own accord? How brown would it have become? Or how yellow?

As dusk fell he reached out and held it gently between his fingers. He looked at the broad expanded blade, the stalk-like petiole, and the veins. He ran his finger along the margin and wondered if it could ever draw blood. Then he lifted the branch, raising it up against starlight and watched the moon against the clouds. In the distance he could hear the laughter and the fires of the town, cries in the night, gongs, firecrackers.

And so he stood, for three days and for three nights. At times he was aware that people had come to watch the sight of the man and the leaf, but he neither turned to greet them nor acknowledged their presence. Well-wishers left bowls of rice and cups of water but it was strange to eat and drink. All that he needed to do was to hold on to the leaf, examining every pore, stroking the sheen between his fingers, testing the firmness of its stalk, watching it age.

Was the transience of the leaf his life or an image of beauty held in a moment, a glimpse of the perfection of heaven? He understood now why he had been sent to think on these things, and that they were both ridiculous and true at the same time.

On the fourth day he decided that he was ready to let go.

He did not know why he had chosen this day. Perhaps the day had chosen him. He took his hand away, and, almost immediately, the leaf fell, turning gently in the air, landing on the grass.

He looked at it lying on the ground for another hour.

Then he picked it up and took it to the monk.

ಬಬ

At the caves K'otan, the chief priest, was greeting pilgrims with the image of the Amitabha Buddha.

'He who desires by meditation upon Buddha and by performance and austerities to obtain birth in the Pure Land, let him first in a clean place put this holy image, with a due portion of perfumes and flowers as his offering. Whensoever he comes into the presence of the holy one let him with undisturbed heart lay together the palms of his hands, put away all distraction, and bend his will to the task of calling upon Amitabha's name, doing reverence, saying, *Praise to Amitabha Buddha of the Region of Sukhavati, maker of the forty-eight vows, the Great Merciful, Great Compassionate . . .*'

Although Paolo wanted to consult Chen's father, he could see that the way was blocked with pilgrims.

'Say it ten times,' K'otan instructed. '*Praise to Amitabha Buddha of the Region of Sukhavati, maker of the forty-eight vows, the Great Merciful, Great Compassionate . . .*'

Paolo began to chant.

'Now give praise to the Great Merciful, Great Compassionate ones of the Sukhavati Region and of the various holy Bodhisattvas and to all sages and saints.'

Paolo gave praise.

'Now concentrate all your thoughts upon repeating the name of the Amitabha Buddha ten thousand times.'

Ten thousand! How long would that take? Three hours? Four? He wanted to see Chen's father but the other pilgrims had already begun.

Paolo wondered if he could slip away once they had achieved trance.

He began to say the name, repeating it so often that he almost fell asleep. When he came to he found it hard to concentrate on what he saw, but the other supplicants were now all in a state of deep meditation.

'Now let us say the name of Avalokitesvara, Mahasthamaprapta, and the holy Bodhisattvas one hundred and eight times.'

For Paolo, this was enough.

'By virtue of this invocation and repetition of the name of Buddha your merit will be abundantly increased and throughout the planes of existence all sentient beings will desire to hear the Good Voice, and will learn the Right Invocation, and be born again in the land of Amitabha.'

Paolo didn't know if he wanted to be born again in the land of Amitabha, or travel for forty-nine days on the back of a white-plumed crane to be judged by King Yama. All he wanted was to see Chen's father.

He uncoiled his legs, stood up, and skirted around the back of the pilgrims.

It took him over an hour to find his way through the caves and he was relieved when at last he saw Chen's father again, sitting alone, eating rice.

The monk handed him the bowl and Paolo took a few grains. 'You have seen the leaf?'

'I have.'

'And you have learned from it?'

'I have learned that my life is as a leaf. That it clings to the tree. It can be ripped away from it, or it can grow, wither, and fall.'

'And when it falls?'

'It falls.'

'And what have you learned?'

'That death gives life its beauty.'

The monk said nothing.

Paolo waited. 'What must I do now?'

'Still such a rush.'

'I want to know.'

'Take out your sack,' said the monk. 'And lay all that you have before me.'

'You require offerings?'

'I require nothing. Just explain what you have.'

Paolo emptied his sack and laid his goods on the ground, as if he were trading for Jacopo. The possessions seemed small and vain in front of a man who had forsaken society. A water bottle. Cloth. Pieces of lapis. A knife. And the leaf.

'This is all that I have. This is what I travel with,' said Paolo.

'And if you could keep one thing, what would it be?' asked the monk.

Paolo knew that he should probably say 'the leaf' but it was too obvious an answer. He looked at the lapis.

'I cannot decide.'

The monk smiled.

'Then keep nothing.'

'I can imagine what it must be like to live with nothing,' answered Paolo. 'But these possessions are memory. I do not keep them for worldly reasons, because I want to use the wealth that they may bring, selling them at a profit at a later date; nor do I keep them for show, as a sign that I have travelled and made something of my place in the world. I hold this stone because my beloved, Aisha, held it. These items connect me to my friends, to my past, and to all that I have been. To rid myself of everything I have would be to take away my former lives and selves, both good and bad, casting away my past and the things that I have loved. If you ask me to live without such things then you are asking me to live without memory.'

'I understand,' said the monk. 'I left my home too, and moved to a monastery where everything was new. A rich merchant had forsworn the vanity of the world and given all that he had to found a place in the hills. The rice bowls were of the most perfect lacquer, each intricately decorated. The meditation hall held a thousand candles that were lit afresh each morning. The scarlet curtains billowed in the wind and were made of the finest silk. The walls were bare but perfectly smooth, unscarred by time. The wind struck against the clean stone but it stood firm, solid in its beauty. And yet this was a place without history. I could not feel the prayers of those who had gone before. There were no indentations on the steps, no footprints of those who had lived and prayed and died. The building had no past. And so I did not feel at home. It was too perfect: a place of serenity and peace, but one which had not been earned. The beauty had been purchased rather than won. Do you understand?'

'You think that stillness only comes after a sacrifice, when we renounce. It cannot be given simply.'

'Exactly.'

Paolo continued. 'You cannot pray without doubt, love without fear, or live without the past. There is no such thing as a new life without an awareness of the past; cleanliness without forgiveness; redemption without the knowledge of sin.'

'It takes time to change. To live without. Could you live, for example, without your spectacles?'

For the first time Paolo was surprised. He had not thought of the spectacles as a possession but as a need; they had become a part of him

'All my life I have not been able to trust the things that I see. They have been too far or too close; and I have had to guess. Now I can see clearly, I still find that I must be suspicious of sight. But I long to return to the mines of Badakhshan and see my love through these lenses, to know that her beauty is as true from afar as it is when seen closely. This is my hope.'

'You live for love?'

'I do.'

'But even love is a possession. You must anticipate its loss.'

'But if I do then I die every day.'

'Whether it is memory, history, love, or desire, you cannot hold on to the cares of the world. You must give them away when you die; why then do you not give them away while you live, and lead a different life?'

'Because there is little point in our being born if we choose to live outside the world, trading the present for the future.'

'By keeping your possessions you are keeping all that has troubled you. Even the lapis that you hold so closely.'

'They are all that has made me what I am.'

'The greatest possession is health, and the secret of life is simple: contentment is the greatest treasure. Confidence is the greatest friend. Nirvana is the greatest joy.'

'I know this but I do not trust it. I am afraid of giving up all that I have.'

'But are you at ease with what you have? Are you at peace with yourself?'

'No,' Paolo replied. 'I am a prisoner on this journey separated from all that I love.'

'Then you are already cut off from that which most enslaves you.'

'And that which is me, that without which I cannot live. Do you not understand it?'

'Of course I understand,' said the monk. 'But you must understand that until you learn that there is, or at least that there will one day be, no "Me", then you will never be at peace.'

'Then why was I born? Surely I must do something, love something, and leave the world better than when I found it. Why was I born if there is no need for me?'

'Is there a *need* for anything?' asked the monk.

 roa

Soon it would be time to leave, but Paolo noticed that neither Salek nor Jacopo was in any great haste to depart. He began to worry about Simone, his commission, and their promise. Did the discovery of such a perfect blue mean nothing?

Paolo also saw that over the last few days his guardian's enthusiasm for jade had been exhausted. Although Jacopo was ready to return, the prospect of repeating such a long journey seemed daunting. He needed more time to gather his strength. He moved slowly, and Paolo noticed how he appeared paler, even smaller. Although this might have been the power of his spectacles, Paolo also observed that Jacopo's lips contained the faintest tinge of blue.

'Those lenses you wear in front of your eyes,' Jacopo complained, 'they make your sight better but mine worse.'

'What do you mean?' asked Paolo. 'Tell me.'

'Sometimes I see the blue of the sky reflected in them, or my own face, but then when I look back the colour is no longer so clear and the world begins to turn. I do not see so well. My eyes are tired, my head aches.'

'You must rest,' replied Paolo.

'My chest too is bad.'

'Your chest is always bad,' said Salek.

'But I feel it: in my heart.'

'It is worry,' Salek replied, 'and digestion. You think too much. Money, jade, travel, weather. And you are missing your wife.' He shrugged. 'This is enough. What comes will come.'

But two days later, as they sat eating their evening meal, Jacopo suddenly stopped and pushed back his plate.

'I can't eat any more. Perhaps I should conserve my energy for Pesach. It will soon be here.'

'You have lost your appetite?' asked Paolo.

'No. I feel giddy, uncertain, as if I have the falling sickness.'

'It is your sight again?'

'No. I do not think that it is.'

'You have eaten too quickly,' said Salek. 'It will pass.'

'Perhaps you need lenses like mine,' said Paolo. 'I will ask Chen.'

'No,' said Jacopo, 'it is not that.' His voice seemed far away and he looked out into the distance.

Paolo began to worry. 'What is wrong?'

'I don't know.'

Jacopo tried to rise from his chair but then fell back. 'I can't find my balance.' Surprised by this unsteadiness, he attempted to raise himself once more. Again he could not stand up, as if the energy had left his body. Embarrassed by his failure, Jacopo now began to pretend that he had never wanted to get up in the first place, that nothing had happened. 'It will pass. Leave me. Let me rest.'

'You look pale.'

'I said it would pass.'

But it did not. Jacopo began to rub at his heart. 'The sky is turning.'

'What is wrong?'

'I do not know. Perhaps it is something I have eaten. My heart aches.'

'Lie down,' said Salek. He stood up and tried to persuade Jacopo to move.

'I am not sure if I can.'

'Come, rest. Let us take you inside.' Paolo and Salek each took an arm and tried to pull Jacopo from his chair. But as they did so, his legs gave way and his body turned in on itself, convulsed with pain. The force of the attack began to radiate away from the heart up into the chest and neck, so that Jacopo's head stretched out and his lungs filled with a surging sensation. He closed his eyes, unable to do anything but let the intense heat possess him.

'The fire,' he said, 'the fire inside me.'

'Water,' said Salek, 'I will fetch water.'

But when he let go Paolo could no longer support their friend. Jacopo's body began to twitch and shake. His arms flailed, and he started to strike out, as if fighting off demons who had come to claim him. This tightly controlled man, impeccably dressed and never hurried, was caught in the dark savagery of pain.

He staggered forward, the world turning around him, clutching his heart with one hand while his other arm stretched out like a blind man finding his way.

'What can I do?' asked Paolo.

'Help me,' Jacopo gasped.

Salek returned with a jug of water and was about to pour it out when Jacopo fell to the ground. He turned over, onto his stomach, trying to grind his pain into the earth.

'Hold him,' said Salek. 'It is a seizure.'

'No,' replied Paolo, 'he needs to be free.'

The body twitched, and Jacopo's head turned to the side, his tongue outstretched, gasping for air.

And then, suddenly, he stopped.

Both Paolo and Salek were caught in the stillness, unable to move.

'Is he breathing?' asked Salek. 'Check.'

'I don't know how.'

Salek knelt down and placed his fingers against Jacopo's neck. Then he felt his wrist.

'Still alive. We must provide ease. Help me to lift him. Let us take him inside.'

They carried him to a low bed and began the long watch over their friend's struggle to live.

ೞ

The first time Jacopo opened his eyes, Salek tried to comfort him. 'Rest, my friend.'

'No, there will be time enough. And that perhaps is a relief to me. I can see the end. I have time to prepare.'

His eyes began to dart, looking for Paolo. 'Where is the boy?'

'Here.'

'I must ask you to help me.'

Salek left to find chervil to cleanse the blood, garlic to ease the pressure, water to cool the forehead: anything that might ease Jacopo's pain.

Paolo looked at the old man, so pale, his beard untrimmed, his eyes exhausted. 'May my death be atonement for all my sins.'

'Why do you need forgiveness?' asked Paolo.

'I have travelled. I have been selfish. We work to acquire and possess, and yet what do I leave? My wife without me, a widow.'

'Live,' begged Paolo. 'Travel. Let us return.'

'I do not think I can do so. I must die and hope for mercy. Perhaps it is good for you to see such pain.'

'What would you have me do?'

'When it has come to pass then go to the Giudecca in Venice and inform Sofia. Tell her that I have always loved her. That she has been my life companion, and that, if it please God, and after the dreadful Day of Judgment, we will be together. Nothing will come between us in eternity. Promise me that you will tell her this: that I die thinking of her, my Sofia, my love.'

His breathing faltered. 'She once hoped that she would never see me dead. At least we have spared her such a sight. Take my goods, change what you can for jade, and give her half. Take the blue stone to Simone. Share the rest of my possessions with Salek. Then do what you will. But, please, tell my wife that I loved her.'

'I will not accept that you are dying. I will not believe it,' said Paolo.

'Ask for her forgiveness. Promise me that my last breath will be of her. Read me the Psalms. I will think of her, and I will think of the Lord who made me and to whom I must return.'

'I promise,' said Paolo.

'You must be the last voice in place of her.'

Jacopo closed his eyes. His breathing was fitful, awkward, as if he could never settle. A slow steady stream of air was taken in gradually over time, the body trembling as he inhaled. He lay dormant, as if already dead, before the breath gathered again for each shuddering exhalation.

Paolo watched Jacopo drift into sleep. He thought of the travels they had shared and all that they had done.

This was what it was to watch a man die.

'You have been a father to me,' he said.

Jacopo did not move. He seemed between worlds.

Paolo watched the effort of breathing: the dry mouth, the sweat on the brow. Dying was such hard work.

Salek returned to the room and Paolo began to read from the Book of Psalms.

He vowed that the Lord was both a refuge and a fortress, and that, even though it failed him, Jacopo's heart was glad. He asked God to show his loving kindness, the path of life, the fullness of joy, and pleasures for evermore. He asked him to keep Jacopo as the apple of his eye and to hide him under the shadow of his wings; so that he no longer feared the terror by night, nor the arrow that flew by day, nor the pestilence that walked in the darkness, nor the destruction that wasteth at noonday. He begged God, through the Psalms, to let Jacopo arise, with angels taking charge of him, and show him the salvation promised to those who put their trust in him.

As the breathing diminished, Paolo prepared the final prayers. He spoke loudly and steadily, as if he truly believed.

'I acknowledge unto thee, O Lord my God, and God of my fathers, that both my cure and my death are in thy hands. May it be thy will to send me a perfect healing. Yet if my death be fully determined by thee, I will in love accept it at thy hand. O may my death be an atonement for all my sins, iniquities, and transgressions of which I have been guilty against thee.'

Jacopo raised his hand.

Was it an acknowledgement, a greeting, or a farewell?

Then the arm fell and his head turned to one side. For a moment it looked as if he had swallowed something distasteful.

He opened his eyes and stared into the distance, beyond those present, beyond the mountains, transfixed on a horizon only he could see. His eyes were dark brown, but they glittered with a terrible beauty. Jacopo seemed in awe of death, filled with its power and wonder. He closed his eyes and sank back.

Still the breathing continued.

Paolo watched the stillness. How pale the body lay. This was the heart of life, the inevitability of death. He looked at Salek, and they spoke aloud, *'Hear O Israel, the Lord is our God, the Lord is one.'*

Then Jacopo gave a long, slow sigh, as if all the cares of the world were fading. It was the last breath of a life.

He died, as he had wanted: like a swan leaving a lake.

This was the fact of death: as simple as birth, as strong as the shock of love, and Paolo was silenced by its power.

Here it was, laid out before him; magnificent, lucid, and distinct.

Salek placed a feather across Jacopo's lips and watched for any last sign of breath.

They waited for eight minutes.

Paolo closed the eyes and mouth.

He extended the arms and hands alongside the body.

Then he bound the lower jaw.

Salek lit a candle. 'The prophet Mohammed kept a Jewish wife, Safiya. The philosopher Maimonides was physician to Saladin. We are all people of the Book, children of Abraham. One day we shall see God.'

The two men watched over Jacopo in silence. There was no sense of life remaining, only absence. The body had been vacated. And in such absence Paolo recognised that mortal flesh meant nothing. The body had been a house, a prison, and a tomb; now it could not matter less. Their friend was elsewhere.

Paolo thought then that the secret of heaven and hell resided not in the afterlife, but in the moment of death.

The only religion lay in how a man died.

VENICE

For the next few days Paolo was haunted by the fact that his life continued when Jacopo's could not. He packed his friend's prayer box, menorah, and shawl; the jade for Sofia; his candles, clothes, and cooking pots: the remains of an existence. Salek took the goods and hitched them to their mules as the women of Tun-huang offered flour, butter, milk, and cheese for the journey.

The men could hardly believe they were leaving and Paolo was filled with a melancholy that he was quite unable to hide. He even tried to imagine his own death. How old would he be? Who else would be with him?

'We all must die,' said Salek, checking their possessions. 'It is only that you have not seen it before.'

'And what do we do now?'

'We continue the journey; we live in sorrow; we try to fulfil that which we have promised.'

They set off through the streets and the markets of Tun-huang, back through the Jade Gate, and on towards the mountains in the northwest. Paolo wondered how the lives of the people around him could stay the same, continuing as if nothing had happened. Did they not know what death meant? Why had life not stopped?

'They have cares of their own,' said Salek. 'If they grieved every time a man died they would be unable to live their lives. We must go on.'

'It is hard.'

'But at least we are alive. You must still learn from life.'

'And what must I learn?' Paolo was almost too tired to ask.

'To leave a person as if you might never see them again; and a place as if you will one day return.'

'The partings seem so different . . .'

'And yet they are the only ways.'

Salek suggested that the quickest route back would be to travel north to Samarkand. They would take the swiftest course, making good use of clement weather and the availability of food, rest, and water.

The temperate climate made all their previous travels seem an unimaginable folly as they journeyed to Bokhara and Merv, and then south of the Caspian Sea and on towards Hamadan, Palmyra, and Tyre. They travelled on, through orange groves and rice fields, past low-lying silk plantations and mulberry groves, riding at last on pale-gold Turkoman horses some fifteen hands high.

The landscape became almost benevolent as they passed the last of the primroses and the first of the columbines, gathering wild mushrooms, mustard, onions, purslane, and watercress, buying buttermilk in the markets, and fishing in lakes and rivers when they could.

At Hajar El-Hubla Salek showed Paolo the quarry containing the largest hewn stone in the world, visited and touched by pregnant women to make them fertile. They walked amidst the cedars of Lebanon, and visited the stone temples of Jupiter and Bacchus at Baalbek. Salek told tales of wonder as they travelled, of spectacular sacrifices, mystical prayers, and secret orgies. Paolo worried if his guide only told such tales to avoid talking about himself and his past, as if the memory of his home was too painful. And, at times, it seemed that everything that mattered – Aisha, their homecoming, the death of Jacopo – and all their fears for the future were best left unsaid.

Paolo thought how little he had known Salek. They walked together and were true companions, but could he ever call himself a friend?

In the Egyptian harbour at Tyre, they found a boat that would take Paolo to Venice. The port was filled with merchants dressed in red and white keffiyehs selling dye from crushed murex shells, glass from Sarepta, cedar from Sidon and Bcharre. The men cried out, offering stone from the sarcophagus of Ahiram, fool's gold, turquoise, sapphire, and quartz. A Frenchman toyed with five civet cats, making them sweat in the heat, gathering perfume from the glands beneath their tails in order to create a scent to attract all women; while an apothecary distilled a mixture which promised to allay the stench of death for ever.

Paolo struggled to remain hopeful, and was tempted to trade here, giving away all their possessions, returning with nothing, as the monk had told him. But Salek urged him to stiffen his resolve, take the jade to Sofia and the lapis to Simone. 'Then, and only then, if you decide to return, the people in Tabriz will know where to find me – if I am alive.'

Paolo sighed. 'Of course you will be alive. I know that I will see you again.'

'Yes,' Salek replied, 'even tomorrow if we are spared.'

'That is not what I meant,' said Paolo.

They watched a group of swifts circle overhead. Salek wondered when his companion would ever learn to take life less seriously.

'Will you return to your village?' Paolo asked.

'No. I have only one more journey; and it is the one which I must make alone.'

'You will live to be a hundred.'

'I do not want to.' Salek smiled. 'When I am called, I will be ready.'

'I owe my life to you,' Paolo replied.

'No, you know that you do not. Only Allah protects a life.'

'I wish I had your faith.'

'It will come,' Salek answered. 'But you must want it to come.'

The next morning Paolo stood on the side of his boat,

watching the figure of his friend recede, and began to wonder if his life could be anything more than an ever-lasting farewell.

ॐ

The ship was a lateen-rigged Venetian trading galley, and, on the route home, Paolo tried to remember what his life had been like before he set sail from Ancona. The memory of that first departure was as distant as child-hood. As they sailed across the Ionian Sea and up into the Adriatic, he lay in his bunk and thought of all that had happened: the friendship with Jacopo and Salek, the discovery of the blue stone, love, spectacles, death.

The confined space made him think what it might be like to be placed in a grave and to lie like this for all eternity. What would his last thoughts be? Would they be of Aisha? Was sleep simply the daily memento of death, given to remind us what it must be to prepare for the final darkness? This is what Jacopo had believed. Every night he had thought of his beloved, death, and his Creator, praying as if he might not live to see the morning. Was that how Paolo's life should now be lived?

As the boat neared Venice, he sensed that he was travel-ling back from his future and into his past. Just as land had given way to water on his departure, now he felt the horizon narrow and the sea become shallow. But he no longer had to guess landfall. He could see the soft green islands of pine and olive, the amber light on the campanili of Torcello, Burano, and Sant'Erasmo. The buildings almost shouted colour: violet, crimson, gold, and green; a panoply of contrast; marble and stone, water and reflection.

Paolo disembarked and tried to imagine the meeting with Jacopo's wife. On the journey he had wanted to forget his duty to discharge the news but now, back in the Veneto, he could think of nothing else. Perhaps he should have sent a boy ahead to inform other family members so that they might tell Sofia in his place. He could picture her sitting down, outside, in a small garden, under a tree; or she would be on the waterfront waiting for the ship to return; or on her way home from the synagogue, at peace with the world.

Paolo wondered if Sofia might instinctively know, if a feeling had come upon her, an unexpected, sharp moment of absence, as if the heart attack had travelled across the face of the earth, and she was aware of its pain. He imagined her in the market, inspecting tomatoes fresh from the vine, stopping suddenly, surprised by a strange intimation, a world stilled.

He paused, tired by the sweat on his forehead, the weight of possessions on his back, the ache in his legs. How could he avoid a confrontation in which a world would collapse, and hopes would be extinguished?

He tried to prepare himself by anticipating every possible reaction to the news: silence, anguish, disbelief, despair: a small dark Jewish woman collapsing onto a bed with grief; a scream, tears, or a long, low guttural howl climbing up from the stomach and being released out into the air, a never-ending screech of denial.

He knocked on the door and waited.

Would Sofia be alone or in company? He thought he should have checked. Now it was too late.

There was a stirring from the room, and he heard the latch lift. The low afternoon sun pierced the gap between the door and the lintel so that the figure was almost blinded by this influx of light.

The woman raised a hand to shield her eyes. 'Who are you?' she asked.

Paolo had forgotten that he would have to explain. 'I have travelled with your husband.'

'What do you want?' Her tone was aggressive and Paolo was unprepared to be defensive.

Perhaps he could leave now, at this moment, before the despair. 'You are Sofia, wife of Jacopo Anatoli?'

'I am.'

Paolo thought he should have found a rabbi. That was how she should have been told: by a rabbi with the rest of her family around her. 'Can I come in?'

The woman paused. 'It is the eve of the Sabbath. You must leave before sunset.'

She opened the door and let Paolo pass.

He tried to imagine this small olive-skinned woman standing by her husband. He pictured the day of their wedding and the two of them eating together afterwards at the table and laughing.

Happiness.

Already the home seemed empty.

It was a simple room with no obvious signs of wealth.

This was what Jacopo sailed and traded for: this home, this wife.

What would it have been like had Sofia been there at the death?

'You have news?' she asked.

'I do.'

He felt hope leave the room. Should he ask her to sit down? Jacopo would have known. Paolo recalled his voice, telling him, protecting him. He had told him the last things to say but not the first; what to say but not the means of telling.

'And what is your news?' she asked.

Paolo sensed the fear rise inside him, the sickness in his stomach, his mouth dry, as if it had been sealed.

There were grapes on the table.

Sofia walked towards them and began to eat.

Now she stared into the distance, eating the grapes, as if, by doing so, she could forestall his news.

Paolo waited for Sofia to finish.

When she had done so, he looked down at his feet, and then across to meet the eyes of this new widow.

'Has it come?' she said at last.

'Yes,' said Paolo.

'He is dead?'

Paolo remembered Aisha telling him about the death of her husband. The rage and the despair.

But Sofia spoke abstractedly, as if she had already joined him. 'I have always tried to imagine this day. Sometimes I hoped that I might die first; that he would be with me. But, because he was older, I always knew that it would be him. It was his heart?'

'It was.'

'I knew that he would be away. That he would leave me and I would not see him again. It would come upon me suddenly. *See, I have set before thee this day life and good, and death and evil.* My life has led to this moment.'

Paolo took out Jacopo's purse and set it down on the table. 'The profits of his trade.'

'I do not care for that.'

'There is jade. It will protect you.'

Sofia said nothing.

'He wanted you to have this. It was the purpose of his journey. Do not deny him this. Take it.'

'Now I hate it,' said Sofia, 'the cause of his death.'

'No,' said Paolo, 'his heart had nothing to do with his trade. It was weak. You know that.'

'But the journey tired him.'

'Everything tired him. Did you think it would never happen?'

'Yes,' she replied. 'Although I had always feared his death, I could never imagine this. I tried to anticipate everything that you have said, but when the moment comes you find that it cannot be imagined. You have wasted that time, feeling fear, imagining disaster. We must live with what we have when we have it. I know that now. I can see it, but it is hard. When you love, you cannot help but dread its loss.'

'And if that fear ruins the love that you have?'

'No,' answered Sofia, 'fear is part of love. That is why it matters. We cannot trust it to last: and so it becomes rare.'

'But it can last,' Paolo insisted, 'at least until death, and then perhaps beyond.'

'People who talk of love are seldom widows.'

'I am not sure,' Paolo began, but Sofia interrupted.

'Was he in pain?' she asked, distracted once more. 'Did he suffer?'

'Only a little.'

She looked out of the small window. 'The night is falling.'

Paolo felt the emptiness between them. 'Where are your children?'

'They are coming, later. They too have tried to anticipate this day. And now it has come. *For death has climbed in through our window, has entered our fortress, cutting off children from the streets, young men from the squares.*'

Paolo sat down beside her. 'Even though I saw it all, at times I hope it cannot be true. Even today I believe that I may have made a terrible mistake, that it did not happen, and I dreamed it all.'

'Death has been laid out before us, and yet in another country; so far away that I will never truly believe it. We will expect his return. And so this is but a dream before the next world. All I can do is wait, and hope that this is not the end but another beginning.'

'He died asking for your forgiveness.'

'Jacopo made the choice between marriage and adventure.'

It was the first time she had said his name, and it took her by surprise: the need to use the past tense, his absence. She stopped and prayed, suddenly guilty, as if she had forgotten to do so. '*May his memory be a blessing for life in the world to come.*'

Paolo knew that he should leave, but Sofia kept speaking.

'Now I have an eternal future to look forward to. A future in which no boy comes to the door with bad news, in which there are no terrible fears or dangers, a future in which our love will last without interruption. Now I have hope again, and our love is no longer burdened by the weight of the past. *The Lord hath chastened me sore: but he hath not given me over unto death.*' She smiled sadly. 'And so,' she said suddenly, 'you were the last voice?'

'I was.'

'You took my place?'

'He was as a father to me. He asked me to tell you that he had never loved anyone as he had loved you. When I had finished the Psalms he asked me to stop speaking so that he could imagine you by his side, holding him, telling him that all would be well. Even if you were not there, he died by your side.'

Sofia nodded, as if oddly satisfied. 'I would like to lie down now. I will let the darkness fall. Then I will light the candles to welcome the Sabbath.'

She stood up. 'Visit me again. Tell me old tales. But do not fear. This is the world. I will not anguish about its ways.'

Paolo stepped back. 'You have shown me the beginning of mourning. You have taught me how love can outlast death.'

Sofia looked out from the gloom. 'It is only the beginning. This world passes. But my husband would have been glad to know you. I am happy that you were with him. *This is my comfort in my affliction . . .*'

Paolo reached out and she took his hand, clenching it in hers, so tightly that even in the gathering darkness he could see the veins rise.

'Go now,' she said. 'Travel well. And trust in love.'

ನಲ

Paolo took a boat across the lagoon and felt the rhythm of the water beneath him once more. Soon his *sandolo* passed the scattered shipyards of the Arsenale.

The frigates, galleys, and brigantines lay stilled in the docks. Paolo remembered the last time he had set out: a confusion of masts, cables, sails, anchors, rudders, and oars; the striking of iron, the heaving of ropes, and the dragging away as the sails were hoisted above him.

Again he thought of Aisha. Perhaps it was absurd to live so extensively in the past, to let the thoughts circle, but such was the strength of desire. Once more he remembered her eyes half closing as she kissed him, the way her breathing changed, the moistness on the upper rim of her lips.

The boat now began to head out towards Murano. He tried to anticipate the joy of his return, to make the memories disappear but they crowded in: the curve of Aisha's back, the splay of her chest, the sudden and desperate feel of her arms pulling him in, and then the rounding, surging, sheer pulse of living. It would never leave him, he thought, and there would never be such intensity again – the undulations of touch, and smell, of taste, and sight, and sound.

He thought of her caress, in the half-waking, half-sleeping darkness, the great joy of life defining hereness and the knowledge that it was the only thing that mattered; that this was all he wanted: closeness, safety, the utter feeling of belonging. It is for this, he thought, for love, that people hope and dream, risk their lives and die.

As he returned to his parents, he wondered how they could ever know what he had seen and done. He tried to imagine what his mother would be doing: gathering wood, preparing food, or sewing, outside, in the street.

Seeing the details of the buildings in the distance, the clarity of the light on the water, and the crowds of people made him anxious. He was frightened by a swift starting up in front of him, saddened by the age lining the face of a beggar, and surprised by a blind man coming round a corner. Everything appeared equally important: the distant chimneys, the stone palazzi, the wooden bridges. He no longer looked through an early-morning mist. The veil of the city had been lifted and here it stood, louder, clearer, brighter than he had ever remembered.

Paolo walked slowly past the boatyard, taking in the colours of the stone, the hard reflections on the water.

He turned into the street of furnaces. Everything was so clear that he did not know if he could continue. His head hurt; his eyes felt heavy, tired by the weight of looking. Then he saw the balcony of his home, jutting out above the street, and the light of the flames within.

He stood in the doorway and watched. The *stizzador* was stoking the furnace. In the distance his father was blowing glass, twisting it at the end of a rod. Now that Paolo saw Marco clearly he was no longer as large and as swarthy as he had been in his imagination, but older, sadder, and more tired.

The man looked up briefly and then returned to his work.

'Father,' said Paolo.

Marco looked up again and squinted. His shoulders were hunched in defeat and the smoke on his besmirched face looked more like carelessness than defiance.

'Father.'

'Paolo? Is it you?'

'It is.'

'Teresa,' Marco called, putting down his blowpipe as if he had been declared guilty of crime. 'Come down.'

'Not now,' she called.

'Now.'

Paolo could hear his mother on the stairs. He saw her feet, then her skirts.

'What is it?' Teresa called.

As soon as he heard her voice Paolo felt his childhood return.

Teresa stopped at the foot of the stairs, irritated to be interrupted. She looked at her husband and brushed the flour from her hands.

'See,' Marco announced.

Paolo noticed the sweep of hair across Teresa's forehead and the pale blue of her eyes. Even at a distance he could tell the sadness.

'Mother.'

She walked slowly towards him, stretched out her right arm, and touched his cheek. 'Is it you?' She took a step back, as if checking every part of him.

'Yes.'

'And you are alive?'

'I am. This is no dream.'

Teresa threw herself around him. She embraced him so fiercely that Paolo wanted to push her away but his mother held on tightly, speaking fast and low, telling him how she had longed for this day, that she had never thought it possible that he would ever return, that she had feared for him, daily and nightly. She had dreamed of storms and tempests, starvation and drought, war and famine, imagining his death, attending his funeral. She had filled her life with fear and had found no rest. All had been anxiety and suffering for she was nothing without his love; nothing without the knowledge of his safety. Life without him had no meaning; it was like a cold furnace that could never be re-ignited.

'I am home now,' Paolo said simply.

'Never leave me again.'

Teresa looked at him once more, and touched his spectacles. 'What are these? Do they make you see?'

He looked at the wrinkles on her forehead. 'They do.'

Teresa stood back, touching a wisp of her hair, oddly embarrassed. 'Now you can tell how old I am.'

'You are still my mother.'

Teresa paused, struck by the memory of his first discovery: the boy in the water. 'I am, I am.'

She kissed Paolo's cheeks, his forehead, and then his lips.

Now Marco spoke. 'You have changed, Paolo. You are a man.'

'I do not know what I am, but I know that I am not the same.'

'And you can see?'

'Clearly.'

Marco stretched out his hand. 'Can I look?'

Paolo took off his glasses and handed them to his father. The world softened once more. The glass-workers moved as shadows in the darkness, lit only by the light of the furnace.

This was how he remembered it all.

He looked back at his parents, standing side by side, examining his spectacles.

'I never thought you would return. Never,' said Teresa. 'But I always hoped, and I prayed. Now such prayers have been answered.'

'And you can see through these?' asked Marco.

'I can.'

'But the world turns. It is like being underwater. Is this how you saw before you had them?'

'I do not know.'

Marco handed the glasses to his wife. 'Look.'

Teresa looked through the lenses at her son.

She could see several faces, all smiling at her. 'Paolo.'

She clasped him to her once more. 'Now I am happy. Now I can die.'

'Do not say that.'

'It's true. All that I have hoped for has come to pass.'

இஇ

That night, as Teresa prepared their evening meal, Paolo found that his glasses steamed up in the heat. He had to keep taking them off and polishing them clear with his shirt. Each time he did so, Marco slapped him on the back and laughed, miming the way Paolo blinked in order to see.

'Like an owl,' said Marco, pretending to be a bird.

'Don't tease him,' said Teresa as she washed the clams for their fettuccine.

'Why not? I am happy. *For this my son was dead, and is alive again; he was lost, and is found.*'

When they began their meal, Paolo stopped for a moment, as if trying to remember where he was. He looked down at the antipasti set out before him: *pomodori coi gamberetti, insalata di mare, trota marinata all'arancio.* This was home. What it was to see once more a basket of lemons or a plate of olives, the simple pleasures of the life he had left behind.

'Tell us,' said Teresa, 'tell us of your adventures.'

But how could he tell? Where to begin? Should he start with life in Simone's workshop and the search for colour? Or should he begin with what he had learned? When should he tell them about Aisha, Chen, or his new-found sight?

'I have seen the driest deserts and the highest mountains. I have seen distances so great that I have thought the world must have no end. I have seen the most precious stones, the darkest waters, and the clearest skies. I think I have known love and seen death.'

'Tell us,' said Marco.

'There is so much.'

'We have time,' said Teresa, taking his plate.

But Paolo spoke as if there was no time; and the more he said, the less they appeared to believe him. He spoke too fast, desperate to explain everything he had experienced; and his parents would tell him to slow down, eat his fettuccine and drink the wine from Verona. He did not need to say everything at once.

Perhaps they thought he was mad.

And yet this is also what happened outside, in the streets. Paolo wanted to speak as if he had been silent for years, but the people to whom he spoke could not comprehend the vitality of his experience or the power of his memory. He could not understand why people first longed to hear the excitement of a traveller's tale but then so quickly lost interest; as if they were so content with their own lives that they could not contemplate the threat of adventure. How slow people seemed, how little they had changed. In only two years his friends had been apprenticed, found their trade, married. They thought that they had grown and developed beyond recognition; but they had not altered as Paolo had done. Nor could they see it. They only remembered him as he had been before.

The less they listened, the more Paolo wanted to set forth once more, to live only as a traveller. The skills and the knowledge he had acquired were not applicable; the wisdom he had gained appeared irrelevant. Everything he had done, every risk he had taken, trade he had made, sight he had seen, or conversation he had undertaken carried no meaning. People listened to him as an exotic but distant traveller who could entertain but who had no value or importance.

He was a stranger, and he knew that he could feel more at ease in Constantinople, Herat, or Badakhshan – anywhere other than here.

'You are restless,' Teresa observed at last.

'Everywhere I go I feel I must leave,' Paolo replied. 'I can never stay still. And I must return to the painter in Siena.'

'Why must you go?'

'Because I have made a promise.'

'When will you leave?'

'In the next few days.'

'And you have nothing more to tell me?' Teresa smiled.

Paolo realised that she had guessed. 'How do you know?'

'I think I am your mother.'

Paolo was so used to being defensive that he could not think how to tell his story. How would Teresa ever understand? And yet if she could not, then how could anyone?

And so he told her how he had found a love which he refused to forget; a love which gave his life its only meaning.

'And you will return to her?'

'I must. Although I know that I should say I am happier with you.'

'It is not a choice between us. I am older. And I have seen you again.'

'You would let me go back?'

'If I knew that you could be happy. And God meant it to be.'

He looked at his mother and then felt, for the first time, the cost of her love and the price she had paid. Perhaps he had been able to leave in the past because he had never been able to look closely into her eyes as a child, or see her clearly. But now, with age and spectacles, Paolo recognised how vulnerable Teresa had become, and that he loved her more than he had ever done before. He wondered if perhaps Aisha had taught him this – to love his own mother. 'I do not want to upset you.'

'Perhaps you hurt me by staying, denying your own happiness.'

'I do not know that I would be happy. But I know that I will have no rest until I see Aisha again and learn what this love has meant.'

'Then you need only my blessing.'

'And I have that?'

'Always.'

SIENA

Paolo had become so familiar with travel, arrival, and departure that his life still possessed the quality of dream. He took a horse and rode south through Padua, Ferrara, and Bologna, and over the foothills of the Apennines. The farmers had begun to cut away at the wheat and the barley as women looked to gather the second crops of olive and lemon. Grapes lay fermenting on the rooftops throughout the route south and he was offered wine wherever he travelled: Moscadello, Vernaccia, and Vin Santo poured from barrels of Slavonian oak. Vintners told him that there was nothing finer than the sangiovese grape; held up to the light, in a fine glass, the colour was richer than rubies. Paolo studied the blood-red liquid, drank, and rode on, looking out over long vistas of hill, farm, vineyard, and settlement. The land was more fertile than any he had known, replete with olives, vines, and cypress trees.

He was proud of the sheer fecundity of the countryside,

far from the arid heat of the desert or the endless expanse of the ocean. He savoured the air and the breeze as he rode, the scent of wild garlic, myrtle, and lavender; and he loved the way in which the spread of the pine trees echoed the contours of the hills above them. Each time he stopped to rest he would examine the faded silver of their bark, yearning for light. Under the topmost canopy of sharp green leaves, the branches thinned into a filigree of lace, supporting each cluster of cone, arching away like all the generations of the world.

He rode through valleys and vineyards, crossing the River Arno to the east of Florence until at last he could see the city of Siena clearly in the distance, rising on the hillside as if it were a part of the landscape. Paolo felt strangely at ease, benevolent on seeing such a home once more, as if no danger could touch him.

He could see the cathedral and the tower of the Palazzo Pubblico standing proud against the skyline and re-membered the great Campo, its slope and rise, the horses tethered by the market stalls, the hammering of black-smiths, the shouts of children, and the mountebanks hawking miraculous cures. He stooped to take water from a well and began to think what the city had meant to him in the past: its strength and elegance, its trade, its people, and its faith. He remembered the gold altarpiece dedicated to the Virgin in the cathedral and the sad-eyed devotions of widows praying in the candlelight, their gnarled hands clasped together as tightly as those of children trapping butterflies.

He remembered the pride of young men parading through the city, hoisting the flags of each district and throwing them into the air on the feast of the Assumption, the cloth unfurling against a clear blue sky to the sound of the drums below.

In the evening light Paolo could see women calling to their children from high windows as the swifts circled over the Campo. He knew this place: the resolution of its stone, the smell of earth and paint, wood smoke from the blacksmith's forge, sweat on the horses, the crowded streets emptying as night fell.

And then, as he approached the workshop, he remembered the absurdity of Simone's velvet doublets and the way he would scent himself with rosewater against the stench of the streets, his head held proudly high; and he recalled how easy it had been to forgive such vanity because of Simone's zest for life, his sudden smile, and the upturned corners of his mouth before he laughed. Now, with his spectacles, he would be able to see that smile dawn.

As he neared the narrow courtyard of the workshop, Paolo realised that if there was one person he had looked forward to seeing again it was Simone. The painter would be pleased, proud even, without ever knowing what such a journey had meant.

Paolo stopped and breathed out slowly, savouring the moment, wanting this sense of achievement to last, journey's end. He realised that he was happy, here, now, in this city, carrying the lapis lazuli to his friend.

Now he could see the panels of poplar stacked under

the eaves, the sacks of lime, the barrows, buckets, and bottles, work in progress.

He thought he could hear a voice calling for pigment, and woke from his reverie, frightened that he might be discovered waiting, as if he had done something wrong. He unlatched the door and pushed it open to reveal his former world, a workshop of paint and gold.

To his right he could see Simone hunched over a series of small bowls, inspecting their contents, examining each grain. 'What a fine vermilion,' he cried.

Paolo saw that Simone's hair had grown almost ridiculously long, that there was a splash of pigment on his right cheek, terre-verte perhaps, and that his hands were more delicate than he had remembered.

He watched and waited. Then one of the apprentices cried out.

'Paolo.'

At last Simone looked up. Distracted from his concentration, he was almost annoyed, as if, for a moment, he had entirely forgotten his former pupil. Paolo put down his bag and opened his arms. Simone rose from his chair without a word, and walked across the room to embrace him.

'Where have you been, boy? I have nearly finished.'

'I have travelled to the ends of the earth.'

'And yet you live.'

'I do.'

Simone could scarcely believe it. Paolo wondered how long it would take him to ask about the stone. He wanted to wait, but realised that he could not do so. 'I have found it.'

The painter looked surprised, uncertain. 'And what have you found?'

For a moment Paolo stopped. Surely he could not have forgotten? Or was he joking?

'The stone. The blue.'

Simone raised his hand to his head in mock astonishment, pretending he had suddenly remembered. 'You have? Then let me see it,' he exclaimed. 'But what have you got on your face?'

'Later.'

'No, tell me now, tell me everything.'

Paolo unfolded his knapsack and picked out a piece of lapis. 'Look.'

Simone picked it up. 'Is this it?'

'Don't sound so disappointed.'

Simone tried to scratch the stone with his fingernail, testing its durability. Then he took it into the light. 'Like azure, only paler.'

'It is pale now but I know that it can yield colour,' said Paolo. 'I have ground it down and I have seen it polished. This is not azurite or indigo, but the truest blue you longed to see. We will turn stone into pigment, paint into eternity.'

'I can see the silver in the blue, and the gold. But the stone seems chalky. Look at the white.'

'Crush it. Wash it. And separate it. Then mix it with tempera. The colour is not as it seems.'

'Do you think so?'

'Trust me.'

Simone placed the lapis in a bronze mortar which he then covered to prevent the dust escaping. He took a heavy pestle and pounded the stone, breaking it into small fragments of shattered blue, flecked with silver and gold. Then he transferred the pieces into a smaller mortar and pulverised the stone until it was ready to sift.

'It needs to be as refined as possible, finer than flour. We must make it last.'

He placed a sieve over a brass bowl and scooped in the mixture, letting the powder fall, blue against gold. He repeated these actions four times, pounding and sifting, coaxing the colour, as if seeking the heart of the stone. They would create ultramarine – sea, sky, and eternity – as if it were the last missing colour on earth.

Simone took another bowl and placed it over a low flame. He asked Paolo to measure out six ounces of pine rosin, three ounces of gum mastic, and three ounces of new wax for each pound of lapis lazuli. These were then blended, stirred, and mixed together over the heat until they melted.

'We will make batches combining this mixture with the powdered stone,' said Simone. 'As this cools let us start another.'

They began to pound the stone again, breaking the colour, releasing the blue. When the gum mastic mixture had cooled they strained it through a white linen cloth into a glazed washbasin. Simone asked Paolo to coat his hands with linseed oil and work the lapis powder and the gum mastic together into a dough, as if this blue were nothing less than the bread of life. They folded it over and over, coaxing the colour, releasing the violet hue at its heart.

Then Simone added a warm bowl of alkaline water and vegetable ash. This was the lye. He began to pummel and squeeze the dough, his hands looking as if they bled blue blood.

When the lye had turned its deepest ultramarine, they drew the liquid off into another container, and began again.

'Let us see how much we can make. Take seven porringers,' said Simone. 'Lay them out. We will add as much lye as we can to this first bowl, letting it blue, and then decant it into each of those bowls. We will go on until the blue is exhausted. The first washing will, I think, be the darkest.'

'When will it be ready?' asked Paolo.

'We must be patient. Imagine this is a feast, a banquet of colour. It will take time, and it must not spoil. The blue will sink through the lye and settle on the bottom of each bowl. Then, when it has done so, we will drain it, and collect the pigment. Only after it has dried can we add the egg yolks and make the tempera to paint.'

'Do you think it will work?'

The painter smiled. 'I have never seen such a colour. Where did you find it?'

'There was a woman,' Paolo replied. 'She could see

more colour than any I have ever known. She could sense the colour between colours.'

'She could hear it?'

'Can you?'

'Sometimes I think I can taste it.'

When the powdered ultramarine was finally ready, Simone cracked an egg, separated the yolk, and began to mix in the powder, folding the paste over and over with a knife. The golden yolk made the ultramarine swell into life, a deep, eternal blue, luminously rich, infinite in density.

Now every memory of Aisha seemed to return to Paolo at once. The first time he had seen her, the stone, and the mountain; her eyes, her hair, and her laugh like silver. He imagined her voice, calling him, telling him that all would be well. Was it the last voice? Yes, he thought now, yes it is, it is the only voice.

'Let me show the men,' said Simone. 'This is how we will paint heaven.'

 infinity

They crossed the square and entered the Palazzo Pubblico, climbing the great marble stairs to the Consiglio della Campana. A large scaffolding structure obscured much of the wall to the east where Simone's assistants were working. Beneath the fresco one man was slaking quicklime, the steam rising around him. A boy carried buckets of water up a ladder and began to wet the wall in preparation for that day's plastering; another cracked eggs for the tempera; while the paint grinder began to mix pigments into ready-made colour: malachite, verdigris, lime white, and *giallorino*.

Paolo looked at the half-finished Maestà, the Virgin and Child accompanied by saints and angels in the Court of Heaven. The fresco was not just painted but carved, incised with coloured glass and raised surfaces. Simone had insisted on inserting glass directly into the plaster as jewels of the Virgin and the Christ child.

The assistants smoothed the plaster over the underlying design, spreading just enough to cover that day's painting, and Simone began to work on the face of St Paul. He balanced three dishes on a low stool, each containing a different flesh colour, and started picking out the halftones of the face, hands, and feet. Then he accented the shadows, blending one flesh colour into another. When he had finished, he turned his attention to the eyebrows, the relief of the nose, the top of the chin, and the eyelid.

As Simone painted, Paolo remembered Aisha wiping the dust from his eyes.

He looked at the fresco of the Virgin, staring out into the world with sorrow and with love, knowing both its secrets and its finitude.

To the left of her throne stood St Catherine of Alexandria, John the Evangelist, Mary Magdalene, and two archangels, Gabriel and Paul. To the right stood St Barbara, John the Baptist, St Agnes, and the archangels Michael and Peter. The four patron saints of Siena knelt below:

Ansanus, Savinus, Crescentius, and Victor, accompanied
by two angels offering roses and lilies to the Mother and
Child, arrayed under a ceremonial canopy of silk.

The people in the painting were stilled, their lives suspended in the great wake of time, rooted in eternity. This
was the reward of faith, thought Paolo, an everlasting
moment of stability and serenity, unchanging, forever
calm, promising nothing less than the certain hope of
resurrection. As he looked at the impassive figure of the
Christ child, he knew once again that this life, lived in a
moment, meant little when viewed from such a prospect.
Perhaps Salek and Jacopo had been right to keep one
foot in heaven throughout their lives, fearing that if they
ever removed it they would lose their place for ever.

'Now, the sky,' Simone exclaimed. 'We must apply the
paint *a secco*, after the plaster has dried. We do not want
to waste it.'

'The Maestà is unlike anything I have ever seen,' said
Paolo. 'Such stillness.'

'And so it should be,' Simone replied. 'Perpetual calm,
an end to suffering.'

The late sun shone through the southern windows,
illuminating the jewels in Christ's halo, the brooch on
Mary's breast, and the tracery behind them. The painting
began to shimmer, for it revealed different secrets
throughout the day, echoing the rise and fall of the
light, everlasting and yet never the same, a continually
changing blaze of gold.

Paolo handed Simone the bowl of ultramarine and

watched him spread eternity over the walls. He had completed his task.

This is how love should be, he thought: a great wash of colour across the blank plaster of our lives.

He let his head fill with the blue and remembered sitting with Aisha, watching the night sky darken.

The painters worked on, lit by candlelight as evening fell.

Paolo walked out into the Campo and took off his glasses, letting his eyes rest in the gathering darkness. The first stars had begun to appear in the sky and the air had sharpened. The square was almost empty; a priest made his way home, an innkeeper tethered his horses, a baby was crying in the distance.

He thought of his life: the days so long, and yet the years so short. What now lay before him? If he stayed in Siena then his future life could all be imagined: paint, gold, ultramarine; the certainty of belonging.

And yet such comfort seemed nothing when set against the rage of love.

Paolo considered what it might mean to leave once more, begin again, and fulfil his last promise. He knew that the truth of his affection was more powerful and more lasting than the familiarity of home. He had tested its absence and found that his life was barren without it.

It was no longer possible to live apart from Aisha. He would go to her and cling to her.

And he would bring up her child.

His life was learning to love.

SAR-I-SANG

He saw Jamal first, playing with a catapult, throwing stones back into the river.

The boy looked up at Paolo and stopped as if he only half remembered him. His eyes squinted against the light. Then he turned and scrambled back up across the scree and stone of the mountain.

Paolo stood below and waited.

At last he could see mother and son emerge from their tent: out of the darkness and into the light.

Aisha placed her right arm around her child.

Together they looked down at him and smiled.

That is my family, Paolo thought. This is my life.

HISTORICAL NOTE

The main inspiration for this novel was the strange conjunction of the coming of ultramarine blue (which encouraged the development of landscape, perspective, and depth in Italian painting) with the invention of spectacles.

The Maestà can still be seen in the Palazzo Pubblico in Siena. It is dated 7 June 1315 and Simone Martini was paid a total of 81 lire and 4 soldi for his efforts.

The lapis lazuli mines are mentioned in Marco Polo's *Travels* and, for much of the Renaissance, the principal source of ultramarine blue was Badakhshan (now northern Afghanistan). The colour was the ultimate luxury, more expensive than gold, and was adopted for the most sumptuous details of a painting, particularly the mantle of the Virgin. When the Florentine painter Domenico Ghirlandaio was commissioned to paint an Adoration of the Magi in 1485 it was specifically stated in his contract that 'the blue must be of ultramarine of the value about four florins the ounce'.

The best early description of extracting the colour from lapis lazuli can be found in *The Craftsman's Handbook* by Cennino Cennini, completed in 1437.

The precise date of the arrival of eyeglasses in Italy is unknown but on 23 February 1306, in the church of Santa Maria Novella in Florence, Fra Giordano di Rivalto delivered a sermon in which he observed: 'It is not yet twenty years since the art of making spectacles, one of the most useful arts on earth . . .' This would put the date at around 1287, which neatly coincides with Marco Polo's reference to the use of eyeglasses by the elderly in China.

Early Italian lenses were not made by glass-makers but by the *cristallieri*, a flourishing branch of Venetian gold-smiths dedicated to working on quartz or rock crystal. This was shaped and polished like a magnifying glass to make convex lenses for the correction of long sight. These 'reading stones' were single lenses, held in a frame made from horn or bone. After the invention of the double frame, probably in Florence in the 1290s, 'eye-cylinders' were born.

Because these early lenses were used mainly for reading they soon came to be seen as a sign of scholarship and wisdom. Tommaso of Modena adds spectacles to his portrait of the Dominican Cardinal Hugh of St Cher at Treviso in 1362; while St Jerome has spectacles dangling from his lectern in Ghirlandaio's painting of 1480. In a Heidelberg miniature of 1456 a piece of inspired anach-ronism takes place: even Moses wears specs.

The development of concave lenses for short sight is extremely problematic, and the current received wisdom is that they took a further one hundred and fifty years to produce. Quite why spectacle makers took so long to realise that if a convex lens could aid long sight then a concave lens might aid short sight remains something of a mystery. It could be due to the difficulties of manufacture. Achieving flat glass that is thinner in the middle than at the edges is quite a challenge. It could also be due to the need for secrecy. Lenses distort normal sight and could have been regarded as heretical alterations to man and woman, created as God intended them to be. Magnifying glasses are acceptable for scholars because they aid the study of God's word. But concave lenses for improved general sight raised suspicion. Some oculists as late as the nineteenth century believed that the use of spectacles with concave lenses might deform the eye (see A. Sorsby, *A Short History of Ophthalmology*, 2nd edn, London and New York, 1948, p. 73).

Perhaps the secret was lost. It certainly seems strange that a concave mirror could be described by Euclid in the third century before Christ and that the Chinese could make both concave and convex mirrors in bronze as early as the first century BCE. (David Hockney compares it to the loss of the secret of concrete, which was known to the Egyptians and the Greeks but 'disappeared' between 430 and 1744.)

It does seem possible that concave lenses were known and used earlier than the fifteenth century. The Chinese writer Shen Kua, for example, refers to concave burning mirrors as early as 1086; and both Alhazen and Roger Bacon were aware of their effect.

Vincent Ilardi has shown (*Renaissance Quarterly*, Volume 29, Autumn 1976, Issue 3, pp. 341–60) that by the late-fifteenth century spectacles could be found to suit most basic visual needs (other than for astigmatism). In *De Beryllo*, written in 1450, Nicholas of Cusa describes beryl as a 'bright, clear and transparent stone to which a concave as well as a convex form is given; by looking through it you reach what was previously invisible'.

Glasses were often categorised by the age of the wearer, separated by five-year intervals, from the age of thirty (concave, myopic) to the age of seventy (convex, presbyopic). By 1462 Duke Francesco Sforza of Milan is ordering all kinds of spectacles from Florence ('one dozen of those apt and suitable for distant vision, that is for the young; another [dozen] that are suitable for near vision, that is for the elderly; and the third [dozen] for normal vision').

The fact that people are even ordering glasses for normal vision shows that by 1462 spectacles are worn for looks alone, and then begin their intermittent history as a fashion accessory. I still find this extraordinary: but then I am one of those short-sighted people who was raised on wire-framed NHS spectacles held together by Sellotape. By the 1960s and 1970s this certainly wasn't a stylish advantage. The brother of my first ever girlfriend once remarked: 'I bet he's no good. I bet he's got red hair and glasses.' This was, indeed, the case.

ACKNOWLEDGEMENTS

I am indebted to Dr Peter Carter who first told me about the importance of ultramarine blue. Nick Sayers, my editor, encouraged the initial idea and I am ever grateful to him. Bridget Kendall alerted me to John Simpson's report for *Newsnight* on the Sar-i-Sang lapis lazuli mine in Afghanistan, and I have been inspired by Patricia Wheatley and Jamie Muir's work with Neil MacGregor in his BBC Television series 'Making Masterpieces'.

Many people have helped me in the writing of this book and I would particularly like to thank the following: Cecilia Amies, Peter and Diana Balfour, Jane Barringer, Mark Brickman, Stewart Conn, Nici Dahrendorf, David Godwin, Patrick Hughes, Marilyn Imrie, Lisa Jardine, Gabriele Jordan, Rosie Kellagher, Emily Kennedy, Olly Lambert, Allan Little, Juliette Mead, Fergus Meiklejohn, Jamie Muir, Susan Opie, Robert Roope, Charlotte Runcie, Tom and Sue Stuart-Smith, Jo Terry, Nigel Williams, and Caroline Wright.

Envoie

from *A Crowne of Sonnets dedicated to Love*

In this strange labourinth how shall I tourne?
wayes are on all sides while the way I miss:
if to the right hand, ther, in love I burne;
let mee goe forward, therein danger is;

If to the left, suspition hinders bliss,
lett me turn back, shame cries I ought returne
nor fainte though crosses with my fortunes kiss;
stand still is harder, allthough sure to mourne;

Thus let mee take the right, or left hand way;
goe forward, or stand still, or back retire;
I must thes doubts indure with out allay
or help, butt traveile find for my best hire;

yett that which most my troubled sense doth move
is to leave all, and take the thread of love.

From *Pamphilia to Amphilanthus* by Lady Mary Wroth (1586–1651)

The Discovery of Chocolate

James Runcie

A story of love, chocolate and a greyhound called Pedro.

When Diego de Godoy leaves his native Seville and takes ship for the New World, he is hoping to find a treasure that will make him worthy of the hand in marriage of the beautiful Isabella de Quintallina.

He finds more than he bargained for.

Fighting alongside Cortés and his conquistadors, Diego falls in love with a Mexican woman and she initiates him into the sensuous secret of chocolate.

From the moment he is separated from his lover, however, Diego and his ever-faithful greyhound Pedro are destined to wander throughout the world and down the centuries in search of the fulfilment they knew for that brief time, seeking the perfection of chocolate and the meaning of life.

Full of excitement, humour and not a little sadness, the drama of Diego's quest is played out against the background of many great cities, by a cast of richly colourful characters, including the Marquis de Sade and Sigmund Freud, to name but two.

The Discovery of Chocolate is a fabulous delight, as rich and exotic as the luxurious confections that Diego himself creates.

'A sensual delight . . . elegantly written and unashamed fun'
JOANNE HARRIS

ISBN 0 00 710783 8